NEW YORK REVIEW BOOKS
CLASSICS

THE JUNIPER TREE

BARBARA COMYNS (1909–1992) was born in Bidford-on-Avon, in the English county of Warwickshire, one of six children of an increasingly unsuccessful Birmingham brewer. Living on the run-down but romantic family estate and receiving her education from governesses, she began to write and illustrate stories at the age of ten. After her father's death, she attended art school in London and married a painter, with whom she had two children she supported by trading antiques and classic cars, modeling, breeding poodles, and renovating apartments. A second marriage, to Richard Comyns Carr, who worked in the Foreign Office, took place during World War II. Comyns wrote her first book, *Sisters by a River* (1947), a series of sketches based on her childhood, while living in the country to escape the Blitz, which is also when she made an initial sketch for *The Vet's Daughter* (1959). This, however, she put aside to complete *Our Spoons Came from Woolworths* (1950) and *Who Was Changed and Who Was Dead* (1954). *The Vet's Daughter* was published in 1959. Among Comyns's other books are the novels *The Skin Chairs* (1962) and *The Juniper Tree* (1985), and *Out of the Red into the Blue* (1960), a work of nonfiction about Spain, where she lived for eighteen years.

SADIE STEIN is a writer and critic living in New York. She is a contributing editor to *The Paris Review*.

THE JUNIPER TREE

BARBARA COMYNS

Introduction by
SADIE STEIN

NEW YORK REVIEW BOOKS

New York

THIS IS A NEW YORK REVIEW BOOK
PUBLISHED BY THE NEW YORK REVIEW OF BOOKS
207 East 32nd Street, New York, NY 10016
www.nyrb.com

Library of Congress Cataloging-in-Publication Data
Names: Comyns, Barbara, 1909–1992, author.
Title: The juniper tree / Barbara Comyns ; introduction by Sadie Stein.
Description: New York : New York Review Books, 2017. | Series: NYRB
  Classics
Identifiers: LCCN 2017024466 | ISBN 9781681371313 (softcover : acid-free
  paper) | ISBN 9781681371320 (epub)
Subjects: LCSH: Single mothers—Fiction. | Domestic fiction. | BISAC:
  FICTION / Family Life. | FICTION / Fairy Tales, Folk Tales, Legends &
  Mythology. | FICTION / Humorous.
Classification: LCC PR6053.O452 J86 2017 | DDC 823/.914—dc23
LC record available at https://lccn.loc.gov/2017024466

ISBN 978-1-68137-131-3
Available as an electronic book; ISBN 978-1-68137-132-0

Printed in the United States of America on acid-free paper.
10 9 8 7 6 5 4 3

INTRODUCTION

THE JUNIPER TREE opens with a children's rhyme, taken directly from the Grimms' fairy tale of the same name.

> My mother she killed me,
> My father he ate me,
> My sister, little Marlinchen,
>
> Gathered together my bones,
> Tied them in a silken handkerchief,
>
> Laid them beneath the juniper tree,
> Kywitt, Kywitt, what a beautiful bird I am.

Although published in 1985 and ostensibly set in late twentieth-century London, Barbara Comyns's novel really takes place in a fantastical landscape, one that is dark, harsh, and dangerous for children and innocents. Among Comyns devotees, *The Juniper Tree* is divisive. Uncanny yet matter-of-fact, spooky yet gentle, naive and knowing, meticulous and strangely careless, it is considered by some to be among her most endearing works, while others dismiss it as chaotic. To me, it's both—and therein lies its charm.

What no one would deny is that *The Juniper Tree* is consummate Comyns, amplifying the characteristics of much of her work. Like *The Vet's Daughter* and *Our Spoons Came from Woolworths*, this later novel features a heroine imperiled by a harsh (yet strangely mundane) world. Its style is a kind of unsentimental magical realism, in which the odd rich detail shines out of an otherwise abstract field. Such details tend to be visual—the "French gilt clock" on a relative's mantel, a ring of "sapphire and two diamonds in a rather old-fashioned setting," a basket of "charming but chipped Victorian china." It's not surprising to learn that Comyns considered herself, first, a painter.

Born in 1909 in Warwickshire, Barbara Comyns and her five siblings had a rather feral upbringing—absent parents, distracted governesses, little in the way of formal schooling for the girls. After her father's death, Comyns attended art school, married, divorced, and lived a bohemian existence supporting her family with a variety of jobs. While working as a cook during World War II, she began writing stories to entertain her two young daughters—and, indeed, all of her books have the quality of dark children's tales.

The Juniper Tree, complete with Grimm epigraph, makes explicit what had only been suggested in Comyns's earlier writing. Bella is a young single mother. Scarred by a car accident and deeply isolated, she lives with her biracial daughter, Marlinchen, behind the antiques shop where she works. When she encounters the wealthy Gertrude and Bernard Forbes, she is enchanted by their happy marriage and welcoming home. The older couple takes an interest in Bella and Marlinchen, and the two small families become increasingly entwined, spending weekends and holidays together, much of them in the shade of the juniper tree in the Forbeses' garden.

Bella is used to rejection, racism, and casual cruelty, but under the couple's attention, she begins to heal from her wounds, both physical and psychological. Where the reader may be suspicious of the degree to which our narrator subsumes herself to her patrons' will—becoming a de facto housekeeper and girl Friday—Bella is pathetically grateful. She seems incapable of agency, yielding to the whims of fate and other people with a passivity that's both frustrating and in keeping with the story's ingenuous tone. In time this passivity proves to be Bella's armor: an oblivious resilience that allows her to weather horror and emerge, like the bird of the Grimms' rhyme, with song intact.

Bella's story ends abruptly, as if the author had lost interest in her heroine. This seeming abruptness is wholly in keeping with Comyns's unorthodox approach to constructing character; in all of her fiction, and in *The Juniper Tree* most of all, there is something deeply haphazard about her powers of attention. Holding her to normal standards of literary propriety can be a thankless exercise—when, for no apparent reason, a character appears and is never seen again, or when another character's personality and motivations seem to change completely from one page to the next.

I suppose it's this random quality, as much as her lack of formal literary education, that has led some people to dub Comyns an "outsider artist." Certainly, it's hard to judge the exactitude with which she has plotted events and red herrings. To my mind, however, it's also one of the chief pleasures of her oeuvre. Very quickly, you learn to stop judging and gauging and analyzing—trying to decide what she "meant" or which details are most likely to come in handy later on—and have to give yourself over wholly to the moment. Reading her is a curiously relaxing experience.

Rather than limiting Comyns, the fairy-tale source of *The Juniper Tree* gives her freedom to invent as needed, and at will. One character may be portrayed with the simple strokes of allegory; in the next moment, we are shown the furnishings of the Forbeses' house and the layout of their garden; we hear all about the meals Bella prepares or the bric-a-brac she restores for her shop. Despite occasional references to contemporary life—technology, feminism, post-1960s sexual mores—this is a world outside normal time, populated by the antiques Bella treasures, and governed by the arbitrary laws of fairy tales.

As to happily ever afters, they are very equivocal things indeed. Joy is balanced by heartbreak. If one character finds contentment, another must pay with her life and happiness. Like a child listening to a bedtime story, the reader is beguiled by the simple narrative tone into a false sense of security, only to find herself shocked by the lawlessness of Comyns's universe.

—SADIE STEIN

THE JUNIPER TREE

My mother she killed me,
My father he ate me,
My sister, little Marlinchen,

Gathered together my bones,
Tied them in a silken handkerchief,

Laid them beneath the juniper tree,
Kywitt, Kywitt, what a beautiful bird I am.

I

QUITE soon after I left Richmond station I turned into a quiet street where the snow was almost undisturbed and, climbing higher, I came to a road that appeared to be deserted. Then I noticed a beautiful fair woman standing in the courtyard outside her house like a statue, standing there so still. As I drew nearer I saw that her hands were moving. She was paring an apple out there in the snow and as I passed, looking at her out of the sides of my eyes, the knife slipped, and suddenly there was blood on the snow. She turned and went into her house before I could offer to help. I didn't like to knock on her door. It was a very private-looking one, painted bottle-green and with heavy brass fittings. Facing the wrought-iron gate was a carved bear with sad stone eyes and snow on its back. It appeared to be late Victorian sculpture but the house was much older, Georgian most likely. I thought I saw a dim figure pass by one of the windows and I hurriedly turned away and walked further up the hill towards the park gates, forgetting that I'd come to Richmond in search of work, not to walk in the snowy park among the deer.

I spent over an hour there. It was a long time since I'd walked in clean snow and smelt its delicate northern smell, a smell so faint it is impossible to describe. Children were tobogganing and sliding down a small hill near the gates. Some had real toboggans and others large trays or pieces of wood. The children were shouting and yelling happily and several dogs were joining in and there was a great holiday feeling although it was a Monday morning in the middle of winter. I noticed a greyhound shivering although it wore a coat, and holding its lead was the beautiful statuesque woman I had already seen that morning. She was intently watching the children rejoicing in the snow, and because of the holiday atmosphere I was brave enough to approach her, even forgetting to turn the scarred side of my face away as I spoke to her. I asked after her injured hand, which was covered by a brightly coloured mitten. She smiled and said the cut wasn't serious in spite of the blood; it was a very clean cut. From the way she spoke I could tell she was foreign, perhaps German. A small boy came running up to us and slipped his bare hand into her warm mittened one for a moment as if to collect its warmth, then ran after his friends. I asked her if he was her son, he had the same colouring, but she said, "No, I like to watch the children playing but have none of my own," and the happiness left her face and I knew I'd said something wrong. She may have had a child and he had died. We parted and I hurried towards the park entrance and the interview I was so late for.

As soon as I saw the shop I knew I wouldn't be happy working there. It was the cleanest antique shop I'd ever seen, indeed there was a feather duster in its owner's hand and she was flicking away at a glass-topped display table. About half of the gleaming furniture was reproduction and the rest well-cared-for antique, quite valuable. The china and glass were in very good condition too, but mostly not to my taste, Dresden figures and Crown Derby dinner services. Miss Murray, the owner, laid down the feather duster and as she came towards me I saw that she was a humpback with a Spanish black shawl carefully arranged around her shoulders and half covering her crisp white blouse. She was very neatly dressed and her tiny feet were enclosed in high-heeled pointed shoes. I felt that she was a perfectionist as a kind of disguise to hide her back, which was not really very noticeable. I told her that I was not a customer and we had already talked to each other on the telephone.

"Yes, yes, of course I remember. You telephoned in answer to my advertisement," she said nervously, peering at my face. "Miss Bella Winter, that was your name, and you said you wouldn't be able to work on Saturdays because of your child. Well, I've been thinking, Miss Winter. It wouldn't do at all, just a five-day week. Saturday is a very busy day for me," and her eyes darted away from my scarred face, then flashed back. It was obvious she didn't want any more deformities in her clean little shop.

Tears came to my eyes as I backed away from her and made for the door. It wasn't only her reaction to my scar, but my feet were wet and cold and I suddenly felt weak with hunger. Miss Murray, carefully arranging her shawl, darted in front of me and stood as if guarding the door. "Don't go, Miss Winter," she said urgently. "You look so cold and I'm sure you would like a cup of coffee. I'm just about to make one. And your shoes. Take them off and dry them by the fire; but remember to put them on again if a customer comes. Now, I was thinking. I have this friend who has a little shop the other side of the river, nothing like this I'm afraid. She wants someone to look after the shop while she runs a stall in some antique market. Would you care to work in Twickenham? It's not Richmond, of course."

Within a week I was living and working in Twickenham. My two-year-old daughter Marline, but usually called Tommy, spent her days in a small municipal nursery just across the Green, where seagulls circled and dedicated people exercised their dogs in all weathers. Saturdays were no problem either because Tommy stayed in the shop with me, quietly playing with the contents of a box marked "Everything in this box twenty pence." Behind the shop there was a large kitchen-dining-room with an antique dresser covered in china which was for sale. Everything in the house was for sale except our beds and a few oddments we brought with us. Upstairs there were two quite attractive rooms, but neglected and shabby. There was a wash-place, no bathroom but plenty of hot water. It was far the best home I'd lived in since Tommy was born.

The antique shop was called "Mary Meadows Antiques" after its owner and was the kind of shop that passers-by often stopped to look in. The early Victorian windows were a pretty shape and the jumble of treasures displayed were more carefully arranged than they appeared to be and there were usually one or two bargains to attract people into the shop. The price of nearly everything for sale was clearly marked. Every morning I slightly changed the window and on Saturday I'd display the things that Mary Meadows hadn't sold in the antique market. I'd worked in several antique shops before but Mary's was the one that appealed to me most, partly because I had more responsibility and Mary was so easy to work with. It was almost as if the shop belonged to me because she only came round about twice a week unless she had something to deliver. She travelled about a lot in her long grey van, picking up this or that at country sales. Quite often she sold things to other dealers before they even appeared in the shop or antique market.

To begin with I never did any buying but combed through the stuff that was brought to the shop by customers and dealers, and if anything seemed suitable made an appointment for Mary to see it. Some of the customers, particularly old ladies, were rather a trial with their re-production brass objects which they assured me had been in their family for years, brass-handled hearth brushes with very little brush, umbrella handles, odd hand-painted china cups, small watercolours, usually of flowers or landscapes, useless bits of embroidery and ugly brooches without pins. I tried to be patient with the people who displayed these objects which they thought so valuable, because some-times they returned with a really good print or engraving ("Sorry, it's only a print"), pretty lustre jugs and mugs and occasionally something almost valuable. I was glad we didn't go in for art nouveau or art deco because neither of us cared for it and it wouldn't have suited the shop. Mary did occasionally buy it to sell to other dealers but not for display.

Mary was small, with curly black hair nearly as curly as Tommy's. Her teeth were small and pointed rather as an animal's, indeed she resembled an animal with her delicate boned face with its merry expression, perhaps a squirrel. She was a darter, darting into the shop with her arms filled with parcels, often wrapped in newspaper. She would pour out a few half-finished sentences, laugh, wave to an ac-quaintance passing the window, rush to the door and with the han-dle in her little paw-like hand, she would give last minute instructions: "Think it has a haircrack; reduce the price if you have to. Richard should call, or is he Roger? You know, the man with the huge ears. And the accountant! I'd forgotten him. Oh, and the Bristol glass walking sticks," and she'd be gone.

On Mondays the shop was supposed to be closed, but if anyone came knocking at the door I let them in and sometimes did a little business. Otherwise I amused myself by painting the living-room-kitchen white and putting a golden carpet on the floor. A cheap carpet made from remnants sewn together and supposed to be washable. I made curtains on an Edwardian sewing-machine all decorated in mother-of-pearl I found in the shop, then sold it for twenty-five pounds although it only had one tubby little bobbin which had to be constantly re-wound with cotton.

Sundays were more or less devoted to Tommy. It was the only day I could give her my full attention. We found a small park tucked away in the back streets, where we could feed the ducks in the stream and roll a large multi-coloured ball down the grassy slopes. At home we'd eat a large lunch, look at silly programmes on television and play with a large Noah's ark I'd bought in a sale. There were dolls too and books; she loved books but the ark was her favourite toy.

When I was a child, just before my father left us, he gave me a large doll. She had rather an ugly face and stiff hair you couldn't brush, but I loved her. I held her in my arms all night and rubbed her plain face with cold cream. One hand was burnt away, black and brown and horrible. Sometimes I thought my mother had had something to do with it. One night I couldn't find her and lay crying and empty armed in bed, but the next morning there she was, sitting in my chair at the breakfast table. I rushed to put my arms around her but it was a wooden box I was holding, with only her legs, arms and head coming out. The square shoulders were very broad and frightening. I threw her to the ground, then, screaming, tried to hold her in my arms again, splinters scratching me from the rough wood. Besides fright I felt a fearful anger, alternately kicking the poor doll, then touching her with careful hands. Eventually my mother had enough of the "joke" and the doll was banished to the kitchen cupboard. Sometimes I would open the door and look at this Frankenstein monster of a doll with its burnt arm, sitting all square amongst the preserving jars, and weep.

I have few happy memories of my mother. She seemed to blame

me for my father's disappearance. After he left us he used to take me out sometimes. There were jaunts on the river to a great palace, most likely Hampton Court, cinemas and ice-cream far better than any I have eaten since. We went to the sea for the day and a lovely woman came too. She came from another land, but spoke English and afterwards I thought she might have been an American. Then much later I heard that she was a Canadian and that she had died before my father was free to marry her. I always remember that outing, particularly because I never saw my father again. After a day with him mother always asked so many questions. If she didn't like my answers, she would slap my hands until I cried—not that she hurt me physically, the hurt was mental.

My mother was the games mistress at a local school which I attended. At first the girls teased me and called me "teacher's pet," but when they saw how she treated me the teasing ceased. As soon as I was able to cross the busy main road on my own, my mother and I travelled to school separately. It was as if we didn't want to spend a moment more together than necessary. Strangely enough, she was remarkably generous towards me in some ways. Although her income was small I was well dressed and fed. At Christmas and on my birthday I was given handsome presents as if they were punishments. I remember a new bicycle once and on my tenth birthday there was a real leather attaché case with my initials stamped on it. No one else at school had such a case. They carried their books in bulging satchels on their backs and looked almost humped-backed as they walked.

I seldom asked school friends to my home. It was a small, impersonal, Kilburn house with stained glass let into the front door and clinkers in the garden. It was furnished with shabby hire-purchase furniture, fully paid for and now almost worn out. The sofa was made of imitation brown leather and when it was hot it stuck to our bottoms, and the dining-room chairs were the same. The general colour scheme was brown, dark green and browny-gold. The only thing that appealed to me in the house was a French gilt clock which had belonged to my mother's French grandfather. It gently ticked away the hours on the ugly sitting-room mantelshelf. Sometimes it stopped at eight o'clock, but not often or mother would have thrown it out. There was Robinson Crusoe sitting under a palm tree and Man Friday ministering to him and there may have been a sunshade although it seems unlikely. I think it was this clock that started my interest in antiques. As I grew older I'd spend Saturday mornings searching for antique shops. Although Kilburn was not a good place for them, there were plenty not too far away and there was the Portobello Road street market, which seemed like a strange fairyland to me. I had very little money but occasionally bought Victorian children's books and headless Staffordshire figures and, on one occasion, a plate to commemorate the birth of King Edward of which I was very proud. My mother suffered the china but later on banned books in case they had "bugs in their spines."

I left school at sixteen with a few O-levels, few ambitions and few friends. Mother immediately sent me to a business college. I loathed it at the time, but the knowledge I gained there has come in very useful. My first job was in a coal office with bowls of coal displayed in the dusty window. It was called "Crimony, the Coal People" and I typed letters to customers reminding them to order coal before the summer ended and the price went up. There were also invoices and the telephone to answer. The women I worked with were kind but elderly and talked about their knitting machines and their retirement. Should they leave their little flats and move to the coast, Bognor perhaps, or would life in a small private hotel be more convenient? No housework, but what would they do with their time? I listened to their plans but knew it was unlikely they would ever leave their safe little homes, at least as long as their health lasted. They were fond of spring-cleaning and gave a day-to-day account of the cleaning as they did it—how the carpet was sent to the cleaners and the curtains washed, the condensation in the pantry and the surprising amount of dirt they found under the cooker and, horror of horrors, the lavatory pan had a crack. Mr. Crimony wasn't difficult to work for although he did sometimes follow me into the basement cupboard where the old files were kept. He'd come very close so that I could hear him breathe and perhaps a dark, hairy hand would come on my shoulder, but that was all. I trained myself to be very quick at finding files, though.

I stayed with coal for six months, then to my mother's dismay went to work in a second-hand furniture shop in Chalk Farm. It was a junk shop really, but occasionally something good appeared, so hopeful dealers came from time to time and I gradually became involved with the antique world.

In the meantime, there was my mother still at the school. Her severe black hair was slightly grey and the slang words she liked to use were a little out of date now and the girls smiled and called her old Winterbottom behind her back. Sometimes she'd have drinks in a popular pub with her fellow teachers, but they never came to the house. I don't think anyone did.

We spoke little to each other, my mother and I. She would make remarks like, "Really, Bella, you look a perfect guy in those trousers. Your bottom is too fat, so are your hips."

I'd say, "Good, that's how I like them," but I didn't. I worried a lot about my heavy hips and legs. The top part of me was almost beautiful and still is except for one disfigurement. My black hair is still thick and glossy and falls into lovely shapes whether it is cut short or left to grow long. My eyes are very dark with a kind of glitter, at least they glitter when I see them in the mirror. My skin is fine and white, a healthy white, and my lips are red even without lipstick. I have good teeth too and a good figure now, but in those days, when I was still in my teens, I was heavy below the waist with a largish bottom, rather thick thighs which bulged a bit when I sat down and plump legs that fortunately did taper at my ankles before they reached my small feet.

If I have boasted about my appearance—and I must admit that I used to be rather vain as a girl—I've been punished for my vanity and given a disfiguring scar on my left cheek. It used to be nearly three inches long, and lifted one eye in a horrible leer, but now, after treatment, the eye hardly notices and the scar is shorter and no longer purple-red. The stitch marks have almost gone too. At first it was as if I had a fearful centipede running up my face and I covered it with my hand when I spoke to people. I still turn the left side of my face away.

My father called me Bella. The name was an embarrassment at that time.

2

I HAD BEEN living in Twickenham for just over a month when the shop bell rang and I hurried from the kitchen with a cup of tea in my hand. Standing with her back to the window was a very tall woman dressed in cream-coloured clothes almost like robes. For a moment I didn't recognize her, but when I switched on the lights, which should have already been on, I saw it was the beautiful woman from Richmond, the one who had cut her hand, the blood dripping on the snow. Her gloves were lying on the counter and as I glanced at her hand she recognized me, smiled and said, "It is completely healed. There is nothing to see," and we stood there smiling as if we were old friends.

She told me she was searching for etchings and good prints and paintings if she could find any up to her husband's standard. She said she had often noticed "Mary Meadows" but this was the first time she had stopped to look in the window. She chose some large and ugly engravings for their bird's eye maple frames and a small print of dogs being clipped under an arch. (The dogs, mostly poodles were tied to a shabby cart. It must have been one of the first dogs' beauty parlours. I think there is mention of one in *David Copperfield*.) She also bought a little chair made of elm, with a heart cut out of the back, definitely a child's chair and much loved by Tommy.

Her car was parked beside the Green and we carried out her purchases and put them in the boot wrapped in dark army blankets to protect the glass. The little chair was placed beside her on the front seat. "I don't want it to be shut away in the dark," she said as if it were a living thing. As she drove away in her expensive-looking car I realized I did not know her name. I hoped she would return. It was as if she were already part of my life.

In the evening, when I cleared the till, there was her cheque amongst the paper money, clean against the soiled notes. It was signed Gertrude Forbes and the Richmond address was on the other side. "Gertrude," I said out loud, "Gertrude," and the second time I said it, I liked it better.

A few days later Gertrude Forbes telephoned and said her husband was pleased with the frames and that she was delighted with the child's chair and thought we might be able to do quite a lot of business together. Then she asked me to lunch to meet her husband the following Sunday. She didn't even know my name and called me Miss Meadows as if I were the owner of the shop. I explained my position and that I was the mother of a child who would have to come with me and she said it was no problem, she and her husband both adored children, "particularly now." I said, "Yes, of course," although I didn't know what she was referring to, perhaps something to do with the Year of the Child. What would they think of my dark-skinned daughter? I wondered.

Marline was the child of a man I didn't know. I met him at a party given in Bayswater by people I didn't know. I drifted there with a flat-mate, a wild Australian girl. The man I'd been living with for over two years and I had parted, in fact he practically turned me out of the flat we shared and I was living in a wreck of a house in Cleveland Square. I shared a basement flat with three untidy girls, mice and some very small but penetrating cockroaches. At the time I was too miserable to care where I lived if Stephen wasn't there. In my heart I knew it was a good thing that we had parted, if I'd had more pride I would have left months ago. Looking back on our relationship, I don't think he had ever felt deeply for me, except perhaps for a short time after the accident. I was the one who loved and he alternately petted or teased me and was sometimes really spiteful, as if to see how much I could take. He complained about my dresses mingling with his suits in the wardrobe, the books I was reading lying about the flat. He said my belongings made him feel hemmed in, "trapped," yet it was he who persuaded me to leave home and move in. We shared the expenses, too, so I cost him very little, the occasional meal or drink out, petrol for the car, the odd taxi, that sort of thing. At times there were painful quarrels over the weekend shopping and it often ended in me paying far more than my share. Meanness over money was a kind of game with him and sometimes he could be unexpectedly generous. It was money that finally broke our relationship, money and the scar that disfigured the left side of my face. Although Stephen was driving at the time, he blamed me for the accident and the loss of his licence for a year for careless driving. He said I distracted him, although I was asleep when the accident occurred. I awoke to find myself lying on the road-side with blood pouring from my nose and face, the blood such a deep brown colour and salty on my lips. Someone was attending to me in the kindest way and I said, "My blood, it's not red any more," and they said something about the street lighting and not to worry. Then I was in hospital surrounded by strangers humped up in bed, some crying out in pain and others as if dead. I wondered why my face was so bound up because the only pain I felt was in my forehead; the other pain came later. Stephen, in a petulant mood, came to see me with his arm in a sling. I was glad his handsome face wasn't damaged.

When I'd been in the hospital for a few days and was clearer in my head, my mother came to visit me. I was surprised to see her bitter face again because we had hardly seen each other since I left home. She produced a large cake I'd never be able to eat, but I could see she had gone to some trouble making it, all iced as it was. Before she left she showed me my face in a small mirror from her handbag and all I saw was a lot of bandages and one black eye. She said in her old spiteful way, "What would your father think if he could see you now? Bella, indeed!" But father was thousands of miles away in Canada and unlikely to see my damaged face. The worst time in the hospital, and perhaps in my whole life, was when they took the bandages away and I first saw the purple seam decorated with stitch marks, the half sneering mouth and leering eye. I'd had no idea that under the bandages my face was like that. When Stephen saw me slinking round the ward with this leering face marked with a purple scar like a centipede he sat on my bed and cried in a stranger's voice, "Oh, my God! I've done this to you," and tears were running down his face. I think he really did love me then. He took me back to the flat and loved me for at least a month. Even my mother was touched by his devotion. It was almost worth having the disfigurement to be so loved. He bought me beautiful scarves that I could drape over the left side of my face. One was made of black muslin with little gold stars on it and another orange and gold, and there were silk squares like the Sloane Rangers wear. I still have some of them stored away.

I dreaded returning to the antique shop where I was working although I'd been happy there. Instead, I became a telephone girl and worked on a switchboard, where no one except my fellow workers could see me—and they soon became used to my ruin of a face. Sometimes I heard them talking about me: "She must have been beautiful before the accident, lovely skin she has," or, "It's a pity about the mouth, her mouth is sort of lop-sided."

When I'd had two operations, the sneer was hardly noticeable and the eye gradually improved. Then the scar shrank and became quite white, but to me it was a fearful disfigurement, particularly on days when I was feeling depressed, and it was then I developed the habit of turning my face away when I spoke, so that people found it difficult to hear what I was saying except when I was on the phone.

I worked with telephones on and off for nearly two years, and after Stephen and I parted I went home at night to dirty flats in dirty houses. Most of them were in the Bayswater district and were overflowing with South Americans and Filipinos, many of them illegal immigrants who worked in hotels. The houses were large and the streets wide and many passers-by appeared to be Arabs. On warm afternoons they sat on carpets in their front gardens, sipping coffee. Sometimes the garden railings were hung with glowing carpets until rain or darkness fell. I never saw the carpets being hung or taken down, they just came and went at appropriate times. They could have been magic carpets.

I moved around the district, Leinster Gardens, then Ladbroke

Grove, then back to Bayswater—to Cleveland Square, which I became rather fond of. I think I had three different flats there—if you could call them flats. They were really large bedsitting-rooms with kitchenette and use of bathroom and sometimes a small balcony looking on to the square. I had one with a balcony soon after Marline was born and she lay there in the sun, if there was any, when the weekends came and we were at home together. During the week she spent her days in a nursery, rather far from the square but near the telephone exchange where I worked. I suppose it wasn't a very good life for a baby but she thrived. Just before we left the flat an albino mouse appeared and he became quite tame and we fed him from dolls' plates. We wanted to take him to Twickenham with us but I felt he wouldn't be popular in an antique shop because he used to gnaw wood at night.

The cottage in Twickenham was the first real home we had had and life seemed perfect, and although it was winter, every day was lovely. With no rent to pay I was quite well off. My largest expense was the day nursery, but my child was well looked after there and I got a discount because we were a one-parent-family. There was a child allowance too, so we were really quite comfortably off and for the first time for over two years I was able to buy new clothes and have my hair cut and shaped by a good hairdresser. I also had five thousand pounds in a building society, which brought in a small income.

For a time this money seemed a curse to me, yet I wouldn't share it with Stephen. It was the insurance money paid for my damaged face. We thought it would be six thousand pounds, but eventually, when my claim was settled, it was only five. For some reason Stephen thought we should share it, although he was responsible for the damage. I asked him, would he have wanted to share it with me if it had been the other way round and he was the one all scarred? We quarrelled bitterly over this money. I didn't receive it until my daughter was born and we had parted, but it couldn't have come at a better time and I was glad I hadn't got to hand half of it to Stephen. Even after we parted he visited me in my first Bayswater lodging and continued the fight. When I told him I was pregnant he suggested an abortion, but eventually went away rumbling like an exhausted thunderstorm. Then I changed my job and address and we didn't see each other any more. He could have traced me if he had wanted to but the prospect of a baby must have scared him. It would be worse than my dresses mingling with his suits. Actually he wasn't the father of my baby but I didn't know that at the time.

I'd almost forgotten my unknown lover. I led a lonely life and had no real friends, just the people I worked with and the illegal immigrants who came and went and seldom opened their doors to strangers, but accepted me. They did things to my meters so that they didn't consume so many coins and they gave me expensive tins and packets of food which I felt hadn't been paid for. A girl from the Canaries unbuttoned her blouse and gave me one of the steaks that were plastered there and I couldn't refuse to take it when they were so kind to me. They were always offering to baby-sit, only I had nowhere to go while they sat.

3

WHEN MARLINE, who later became Tommy, was born I could hear the nurses exclaiming and I thought the baby was deformed in some way, but later, when they put her in my arms, I saw what had caused the surprise. The baby was coloured. She was a dear little thing, but I handed her back to the nurse and said, "You have made a terrible mistake. This couldn't possibly be my child, all dark like this. She's beautiful, but she isn't mine."

The nurses insisted that she was. There were three of them now, all standing round my bed, and a tall thin sister was advancing towards us as if expecting trouble. They showed me the identity bracelet she wore on her wrist and they insisted that I held the little thing and, as I held her and looked down at her darkness, I felt a bitter rapture because in spite of her colour I knew she was mine.

I had been shutting my mind to something for months, something I couldn't face. It happened soon after Stephen and I parted, when I went to a party given by unknown people in an unknown house not far away from where I was living. I went there with this wild Australian girl I have mentioned before, and drank too much or mixed my drinks unwisely and felt sick and unhappy. It was a horrible party, with people lying around the floor, a few dancing like zombies, and queer women wearing evening dress and heavy make up who turned out to be men. There was one woman naked to the waist slumped over a chair with a syringe hanging from her arm.

I was talking to a young negro wearing a crimson velvet jacket. He smelt of dusty velvet and sweat, but he was gentle and kind and, before I became drunk, we had danced a strange dance together. Later on he was telling me all his problems and he seemed to have a great many. We left the party together and I couldn't have been as drunk as I thought because I managed to walk down five flights of stairs without falling. It was wonderful to be in the quiet square with the sleeping cars humped outside the houses like sleeping animals, elephants perhaps, one could almost hear them breathing. The young negro put his arm round me and we walked to the dirty house where I lived and went upstairs together and into my cold room. I remember he kindly put money in the meter and lit the gas fire and I think I made us some instant coffee and we huddled on the divan talking about our problems and there may have been some lovemaking which I can't recall, but I do remember waking in the darkness and finding this negro there and the strong smell of dusty velvet. The next time I woke he wasn't there any more. I never saw him again, although I believe he came round looking for me after I'd moved.

The nurses thought I might reject my dark baby and kept standing within earshot saying things like "Have you seen Bella's baby? She's the prettiest in the ward." Then to me, "Have you noticed her lovely cheek bones and the shape of her little face?" A German nurse who was studying English and nursing at the same time used to call her little Marline or Marlinchen and when the man came round to register the babies' births she somehow became Marline although I didn't care for the name much and later changed it to Tommy, which suited her very well.

Actually she wasn't very dark, just a nice golden colour like ginger snaps, but her lips were rather pronounced and her hair was dark and woolly. Otherwise she was very like some of the South American children who ran in and out of the basement flats of the houses where I had lived. Sometimes ill-bred women remarked about her in buses and shops. They always started with something like, "What a pretty child! Is she yours?" and, when I said, "Yes," they'd smile spitefully and say something like, "Pity about the hair. She could almost pass for white if it wasn't for the hair."

One actually remarked, "It's lucky she didn't inherit that mark on your face. A scar, is it?" I remembered these remarks because they hurt me, but most people loved Tommy and quite rightly thought her beautiful. The nurses need not have worried that I might reject her because, after the first shock, I adored her and wouldn't have had her any different although I couldn't help worrying a little about her future.

Tommy and I both wore new clothes the Sunday we went to lunch with the Forbeses, casual clothes, but new. I had the feeling that it was a momentous day in our lives, that the Forbeses would have a great influence on our future and help in some magical way. We were a little late when we arrived at their Richmond house because it was further away from the station than I remembered. When we did reach it and I was dealing with Tommy's folding pram, she saw the carved bear in the front courtyard and insisted on riding on its back with her skinny legs in their scarlet tights sticking out either side and such a look of joy on her face. That is how the Forbeses first saw her when they came to the hall window, and if they were surprised to see that she was coloured, they never showed it.

We went into the house and it was very much as I'd imagined it would be, rather bare and beautiful, the furniture mostly heavy antiques and the walls white. I was surprised to see the large and valuable paintings hanging on the walls. Then I remembered Bernard Forbes was a picture dealer and restorer and had a gallery somewhere in the West End, indeed there was a workshop in the semi-basement where a young man called Peter did framing and in a large studio at the back of the house picture restoring went on and perhaps a little faking too.

There was a great feeling of love and happiness in the house, and a feeling of goodness too. The food was good and pure, a delicious white creamy soup, homemade bread, various cold meats and vegetables, a salad sprinkled with nuts, several different cheeses and a pudding made with honey, real honey-in-the-comb honey, and fruit. There was wine to drink, red and white, and, although I know little about wine, I could tell it was something special, better than any that had come my way before.

As I'd thought, Gertrude was of German origin but Bernard was

English. Both were tall and very handsome, Gertrude really beautiful with a kind of radiance about her. Tommy, usually a shy child, took to them immediately and they were sweet and gentle with her, carefully listening to what she tried to say. After luncheon, she took Gertrude by the hand and they went out into the courtyard to feed the lion with some scraps of bread—which the birds ate as soon as their backs were turned. To the Forbeses Tommy was always Marlinchen and I found myself calling her by that name too.

Although Bernard was inclined to be a reserved and formal man, I found him quite easy to talk to. We had antiques in common and he knew a lot about the history of the district, including Twickenham. He told me about the famous and interesting people who had lived there and how it used to be before it became so built over. He lent me books on subjects I'd hardly been interested in before, botany, for instance, and architecture. He seemed to enjoy stretching my rather ignorant mind. Even on my first visit he lent me so many books that we had to be driven home in his car. There was even a book for Marlinchen, a Victorian pull-out with animal illustrations, very delicate and unsuitable for a small child, but he insisted that she wouldn't harm it and, as usual, he was right.

Before we left, Gertrude showed me over the house, which was very large and on four floors. Some of the rooms were used for storing paintings; but even then they had four bedrooms, a dining-room, drawing-room, a study for Bernard, two bathrooms, the studio and a big kitchen with natural wood cupboards and a long refectory table with the old greyhound, Petra, asleep under it. There were many herbs in jars beside hanging strings of onions and garlic, and there were other hanging vegetables, mushrooms and things I didn't recognize. Two slightly intimidating cookers stood side by side and there was a huge deep freeze and a scarlet refrigerator. From the windows I could see the long garden, formal near the house, then almost wild, with many large trees and bushes melting into the winter mist. On a little lawn of its own there was a swing gently moving in the soft west wind as if some child were already sitting there.

I cried, "Oh! What a lovely swing, how a child would love it," but there were no children and I felt my usually pale cheeks burning red at my thoughtlessness.

Gertrude turned to me eagerly: "Yes, that's what I've always thought and I've kept it there for fifteen, no, sixteen years waiting for a child and now, by some miracle, there may be one. It is not quite certain, but almost." And, although I didn't know Gertrude well and I don't touch people often, I flung my arms round her and we stayed embraced like that for minutes while the swing moved in the wind.

4

MARY MEADOWS was pleased with the way I managed the shop, so beside my salary and free accommodation she gave me a small percentage on everything I sold and I was able to put money aside. This gave me a feeling of security and pride and it was as if the shop really were mine without the bother of searching for new stock. Mary saw to that side of the business. The customers were friendly too, sometimes so friendly it was difficult to get them out of the shop. The dealers were more business-like and friendly in a different way. Sometimes I went to one of the local pubs and had a drink or cold lunch with them, but not often because it was difficult to leave the shop except between one and two o'clock.

Miss Murray became a customer and would arrive wearing a cape to disguise her back. In spite of her nervous manner, she was a kind woman and quite often directed people to the shop. "People who don't mind the odd crack or scratch, dear. They'll buy anything if they think it's old." She would dart round the shop picking on this or that. "The damask on this walnut chair is in shreds, as if a cat had clawed it. You'll never sell it. Not one of these Ralph Wood figures is perfect. Elijah has a thumb missing. Did you know?" All the same, she generally ended up buying something and I was always pleased to see her, particularly now she had accepted my scar. People did become used to it in time.

Bernard Forbes spoke about my scar in an almost brutal way. He would ask questions about it and, when he knew me better, he snatched my hand away from my left cheek when we were talking together. He took photographs of the side of my face that wasn't perfect with my hair all drawn away. He said the disfigurement was so slight it was morbid of me to care so much; but then he hadn't seen it as it used to be. Often when I awoke in the morning I'd run my fingers over my face to assure myself that it really had improved; but at times of stress I'd forget the improvement and to me it would be as bad as it had ever been and I would shield my face with my hand or hair or anything to hide it.

The Forbeses often came to the shop on Saturday afternoon, just before it closed. Sometimes, if a customer came in, Bernard would pretend it was his shop and go to great trouble to sell some small object—an Edwardian glass shade, or a paperweight with a view of the Isle of Wight inside it, or a steel carving-knife and fork. "This knife will just melt through your joint, madam," he'd say with great conviction. "You'll never suffer from tough meat again," and he would see the customer to the door and gravely bow as they left. The customers always bought from him. It was as if he hypnotized them. Gertrude would sit smiling and watching what went on. She often had Marlinchen on her knee and they would be playing with some small thing she had bought for her. There she sat, pregnant for the first time at thirty-six, glowing with health and looking more beautiful than ever. Mary called her the German Venus and the two of them combined were "The German Giants." Although Bernard had no German blood, he had rather a German temperament, bossy and organizing, but maybe I needed organizing. Gertrude would tell him to leave me alone, but he would say, "I'm helping her, don't you see? She needs to have more faith in herself, poor little scrap."

I had not seen my mother since a few months after the accident, when I was moving around from one dreary Bayswater flat to another, pregnant. She didn't even know she was the grandmother of a beautiful brown baby with a mop of woolly hair. I didn't want my mother near my Tommy, casting shadows and killing love. But Bernard thought differently; he even felt sorry for her and I wished I hadn't mentioned her. Even Gertrude, who usually stood up for me against her husband's teasing interference, felt sorry for my mother: "Just write her a little letter telling her how you are. No need to mention Marlinchen if you'd rather not, but later on she must know. Just write the little letter and put her mind at rest. Think how worried she must be, poor woman."

Eventually they wore me down and, fortified by a glass of red wine, I telephoned my mother, half expecting a strange voice to answer. But it was my mother's voice I heard. "Bella, Bella," she said in a frozen voice, then quite sharply, "well, what do you want? You aren't in trouble, are you?" I assured her that I wasn't, that I was happier than I had ever been and had a lovely job. "Then why did you telephone if everything is going so well," she snapped, adding more kindly, "I did look for you after you left Stephen, I really did. I went to one dirty house after another, Stephen and I both looked, but for some reason he suddenly lost interest—another girl, I suppose. But if you weren't in trouble, why did you hide?"

"There were reasons," I said, "but I can't go into them now. Do you think we ought to meet, mother, or leave things as they are?"

"No, of course we'll meet. What kind of a mother do you think I am? I'd prefer it if you came to me, really; you see I have a surprise for you. When could you come?"

I felt sure I wouldn't like the surprise and it would weigh on my mind until I knew what it was, so I arranged to go the following day, Monday, the day the shop was supposed to be closed—so for once I'd really close it.

On Monday morning, after a worried night, I ran across the Green with Tommy, not even stopping to feed the hungry seagulls, usually a morning ritual. I pushed a protesting Tommy into the nursery and hurried home to prepare myself to meet my mother. I washed my hair and trimmed it with very sharp scissors and it fell all black and shining round my face. I examined my scar, which after two operations and several years appeared to be growing less and less noticeable, and I put on the new clothes I'd worn the first time I'd visited the Forbeses, reassuring myself by looking at the label marked size twelve and not the hated size fourteen. The heaviness around my hips and thighs had melted away and mother wouldn't be able to tease me about my fat bottom any more. My whole appearance had improved since she last saw me, so there was little she could pick on.

It was a long journey to Kilburn by bus and train and with a long-ish walk downhill at the other end. It was an eventful three or four years since I'd walked that way and stood on my mother's doorstep; but now I was a visitor without a key, ringing the tarnished brass bell. The door was no longer blistered and brown but newly painted white. The yellow and green stained glass still remained, though, and brought back memories of my childhood. I'd thought it rather beautiful when I was very young but then I came to despise it. Now I was quite pleased to see it had survived.

I was still studying the stained glass when mother opened the door and I could see she was as nervous as I was and unsure whether to give me a kiss or not, so I gave her a quick peck on the cheek. Then we took an uneasy look at each other and I saw that my mother had changed. Her hair had been tinted to its original black and was cut in a rather severe style that suited her. Her clothes had improved too. She no longer looked the ageing games mistress with shaggy eyebrows and feet in heavy shoes. Indeed, she was wearing high-heeled court shoes and the sheerest of nylons, and her face, though haggard, was almost beautiful in spite of the heavy chin. I said, "Mother, how handsome you look!"

She seemed pleased, but a little embarrassed. "I'm glad you think so, Bella," she said and we sat down stiffly on the cretonne-covered chairs. The chairs were all decorated in red roses and the carpet was a light silver-grey. She must have noticed my surprise. "Yes," she said, "things have changed since you left to live your own life. For one thing, I let your room and that brought in a little extra money, and then your father died in Canada and left me a few thousand pounds, which will go to you eventually. It has been a great help. I've given up the games, you know. I became very tired of the girls. I'm not overfond of children and blowing that whistle and standing about in all weathers was too much for a woman of my age. I'm forty-eight, you must remember. Then there was the gym and those great, sweat-ing girls scrambling over the horses and swinging from the trapeze like a lot of young gorillas. Now I've finished all that and work part-time in a travel agency in the High Road. My French comes in useful and I like the work and there are a few bonuses attached. Cheap travel and that sort of thing."

Above my head I heard the slip, slip of slippered feet on lino, then the unmistakeable sound of a lavatory being flushed. "Mother, who's that walking about upstairs and pulling plugs?" I cried and jumped up from my chair. For a moment I'd thought it must be my father up there, then remembered that he was dead so sat down again and waited for my mother to speak.

"I've already told you that I let your room to a gentleman, Mr. Crimony—you remember him, don't you? The coal-merchant. You worked for him at one time, then threw the job back in his face. All the same, he's always been very friendly towards me, helpful too. Then his wife died and he found that gloomy old flat in Maida Vale very difficult to manage. He seemed very lonely, so I let him have your room. You don't object, do you?"

"Of course I don't object. How could I?" I said crossly; then asked if they had meals together, hoping they didn't. Mother said almost humbly, "In the evening we do and sometimes at breakfast, but of course we are both out in the middle of the day. He specially stayed at home this morning because he wanted to see you, so be nice to him, won't you?" She stood up and ran her fingers through her hair, glanced at her reflection in the mirror over the mantelshelf and tripped on her high heels towards the kitchen. "Stay where you are, dear, I'll only be a minute," she said cheerfully as she left the room. She wasn't at all like the mother I remembered.

I sat alone on the bright covered chair looking up at the ceiling and listening to the soft sound of someone walking in slippers. It changed to the sound of heavy shoes, then steady footsteps coming down the stairs and Mr. Crimony came through the door. He looked brighter and cleaner than I remembered but he still wore the same old-fashioned stiff winged collar and to me he seemed to smell of coal dust. To my horror he came close and, bending over me, kissed me on the forehead. Then he patted one of my hands familiarly. "Well, Bella, it's good to see you again," he said in his deep greasy voice. "What a pretty girl you have grown into! And that scar I heard so much about, it's hardly noticeable, particularly when you are sitting with your back to the light as you are at this moment. But you can't always keep your back to the light, can you?" he tittered.

My mother came in and announced lunch. "Steak and kidney pie. I hope you like it, Mr. Crimony?" she asked.

"Indeed I do. You know I dote on your pastry. I have been complimenting Bella on her appearance. She has grown into a handsome young woman and that scar isn't at all bad. I tell her she must keep her back to the light and no one will notice." And he went on tittering as we walked into the dining-room and sat down to eat our steak and kidney pie followed by treacle tart. No wonder I'd been overweight when I lived at home. Or was all this pastry in Mr. Crimony's honour? There he was calling mother Annie in a most familiar way and she laughed at his feeble jokes. But she did at least call him Mr. Crimony and not Charlie which I seemed to remember was his Christian name. Even when we returned to the drawing-room for coffee he was still with us so I was unable to mention my daughter or anything about my present life. Perhaps my mother did not want to know about it because she seemed quite happy about Mr. Crimony's heavy presence. I suggested we washed up the dishes together; but she declined my help because she had recently had a dishwasher installed in the kitchen.

When we finished our coffee I said it was time I went home and no one pressed me to stay longer.

As I said goodbye to mother on the doorstep I suggested a visit to the shop, but she seemed doubtful. "It would mean a lot of travelling and I don't think I could spare the time." But Mr. Crimony had crept up behind her and suggested driving her over one Sunday. "It'd make a nice little drive, Annie, we could go through the park and cross the river and be in Twickenham in no time. We will be getting in touch, Bella, never fear."

When I got as far as the gate I looked back and they were still standing there, and one of Mr. Crimony's heavy hands was on mother's shoulder. Was he the "little surprise"?

5

THE SPRING came early that year and I walked in the Forbeses' garden with Gertrude, who was looking splendid in a blue cashmere dress, her happiness shining out of her. She said she had never felt so well before, indeed she had no morning sickness or any of the other minor discomforts of pregnancy. Sometimes she said, "Wouldn't it be awful if I wasn't pregnant at all? Suppose it was only a false pregnancy, women do have them, you know."

Marlinchen ran ahead of us to examine the daffodils which were just coming into flower and we'd shout "No, no!" every time her hand went out to pick one—well, not exactly pick, she pulled their heads off, looking at us and laughing as she did it.

The Forbeses' garden must have been the first private garden she had been in and she called it "the park" although it was most unpark-like, as a large part of it was almost wild with little paths twisting between the trees and bushes. There were several apple trees about to blossom and a large cherry. Near the cherry tree in a wild corner there was something Gertrude called the juniper tree, although it was really a very large bush. She said it had berries that she enjoyed eating. "I believe they are used in the making of gin," she laughed, "but I like them." There was a bench where Gertrude used to sit under her tree, watching the birds, and she said that if she were worried about anything, the worries went away. The old greyhound, who followed us, lay down by the seat as if it were a place she was very used to.

On Saturday evenings, after the shop was closed, the Forbeses often took us home with them and brought us back on Sunday night. One of the things we enjoyed about this was using their beautiful bathroom, as we only had a little washroom with a basin at the shop. We really looked forward to our baths there, often using flower-scented, foaming bath seeds to add to the luxury.

That spring Sunday we were enjoying the garden, Gertrude was expecting a visit from her younger sister, Charlotte, who taught in a nearby German school. She was tall and golden-haired like Gertrude, but there the likeness ceased. She had a high colour in her cheeks and an air of authority. To myself I called her the Corn Maiden, and although I admired her brains and strength of character, I was a little afraid of her. She didn't get on with Bernard very well and they argued over the dining-table. This Sunday was no exception. While the rest of us were enjoying sole cooked in mushroom and chive sauce, they were arguing about late Sumerian culture and Bernard appeared to be really angry.

"I wish she wouldn't do it," Gertrude said in a low voice. "She even lays down the law about wine; men hate that sort of thing." Then, loudly, "You two stop, you've gone on long enough," and there was peace for the rest of the meal.

Then, when we were having coffee round the drawing-room fire, Bernard suddenly broke the comfortable silence and said, "Well, Bella, have you been in touch with your mother?"

So I stammered out an account of my visit, aborted by the persistent presence of Mr. Crimony. Now I was sharing it with other people my visit seemed almost funny and not distressing as it had seemed at the time. The pity was that, if the silly Crimony had not been there, my mother and I might have got on quite well. The little improvements in her appearance had touched me and under her prickly manner there appeared to be a faint warmth as if there were a little seed of understanding there.

"So she still does not know about Marlinchen, then," Gertrude said regretfully. "Never mind, the next time you meet things will be better. You must choose a time when that man isn't there," and she patted me encouragingly. "If she only works part-time you must telephone her in the afternoon when the boring Crimony is selling his coal."

Bernard asked, "Do you think he is planning to marry your mother?" I didn't answer because Marlinchen awoke from her afternoon rest on the sofa and demanded to be taken to the swing in the "park," and Bernard threw away the stump of his Sunday cigar and decided to take Charlotte and the greyhound for a walk, so no more was said about my mother. As they left the house Bernard and Charlotte were quarrelling again, this time about a Spanish painter called Tàpies, and Bernard was almost shouting, "Of course I know I'm right. After all it is my job." And their angry voices grew fainter as they walked up the hill.

In the evening, when Bernard drove us home, I saw there was a note sticking out of the letter-box. Customers often left notes when the shop was closed so I wasn't surprised, but when Bernard had driven away and we had taken off our outdoor things I remembered the note and unfolded it to read, "Sorry you were out." It was signed "Mother and Charlie," but it wasn't written in mother's handwriting.

On Monday evening I telephoned her but it was Crimony's voice that answered. I replaced the receiver and tried again a little later. It was Crimony's voice again, but this time I persevered and, trying to disguise my voice, asked to speak to Mrs. Winter. Crimony was not deceived. "Is that you, Bella? Speak up louder, your voice isn't very clear, ducky. I suppose you want to speak to your mother. She's sitting right beside me and she'll be ever so pleased to have a little chat with you."

I could hear whispers, then my mother's voice. "Is that you, Bella? Have you anything particular to say to me? Yes, it was a pity we drove all that way and you weren't there. You would like me to come next Sunday, about tea-time. Or any other day would do. Well, make up your mind, dear. You say Monday would be best for you. I don't think Mr. Crimony could manage Monday. No, of course I couldn't come by bus and train after a heavy morning at the travel agency. You are making it very difficult and I haven't time to go on and on talking. We'll leave it open. Anyway, this line is very bad, I can distinctly hear a child's voice cutting in. Goodbye, keep in touch." And the receiver was replaced.

"Mummy, who was that?" Tommy asked for the third time. She liked to join in on telephone conversations. "Actually it was your granny, though you wouldn't think so," I said as I hugged her close and carried her upstairs. I wouldn't have risked making a call if I'd known she wasn't asleep in her bed. I looked down on the smiling face on the flowered pillow and thought that Mother was exceedingly fortunate to have such a lovely grand-daughter, even if she did not know it yet.

Easter came and the Salvation Army band played stirring music on the Green and then went home to eat hot cross buns. It was a cold, wet Easter and there was nothing much to do. The shop was closed for three days and the Forbeses were somewhere in Devonshire. They were to be away for at least ten days and I hadn't realized before how dependent I was on them. They, and in a lesser degree, Mary Meadows, were my only close friends. How had it happened that I'd become so isolated? I used to be a friendly girl, perhaps a little reserved, but still friendly. I'd been fairly popular at school although I seldom asked girls home. Later there had been the odd boyfriend but men meant little to me until I met Stephen. I longed to be loved and admired but had little to give in return. With Stephen it was different. I used to think it affected when people talked about total commitment, but that was what I had for him, real, total commitment, or rather, the first year we were together total, and the second, just commitment. After the accident, just for a little time, it was total for both of us; but it didn't last long, and he turned away from me as we talked although he had caused the sneering scar to come on my face. Then the quarrels started, usually about money because for a time I couldn't pay my share and when I became a telephone girl I didn't earn much. Stephen seemed to be really pleased when I moved out. This made me more and more bitter and we said such unforgivable things to each other. I think most women would prefer their particular man, the man they love, to be cruel rather than mean. It was small things like, "Could you pay the taxi? I haven't any change," or, "Will you see to the porter, dear?" Stephen had several expensive watches and a carriage clock which was always needing attention and somehow it was always me who had to collect them and pay the watchmender. I'd far rather he had hit me than practise these meannesses on me. Even so, I did miss him the first year we were apart; but as I became more and more engrossed in Tommy Marline I thought about him less and less, and rather pitied whoever had taken my place. But in spite of my child's company, I was very lonely that Easter.

6

WHEN THE Forbeses returned from Devonshire, Gertrude appeared to be a little tired and her heavy lids half covered her great eyes, giving her a doll-like look. She said that she didn't care for hotel life and that she had missed her garden. The garden was looking particularly beautiful. In the wild part that Gertrude called the spinney or thicket, the trees had grown even thicker and the green branches were closely entwined. The birds sang until the trees resounded and the last of the blossom fell on the mossy green and blue ground. At first glance I thought the blue was bluebells but it was wild periwinkles growing in great profusion. I'd never seen them grow like it before. Gertrude said they sometimes did abroad and the ones in her wild garden were descended from a few she had brought back with her from a Spanish wood years ago. We sat on the bench under the juniper tree and she nibbled a few of the needle-like tender leaves as we talked in a comfortable way. We really were happy to be together again. Bernard joined us for a few minutes but did not stay long and refused to share our bench. He preferred the tame part of the garden. Besides, he was practically driven away by a pair of noisy magpies who had built a strange, dome-shaped nest in a nearby tree. Gertrude looked at them and smiled. "I know they are thieves and steal other birds' eggs—and baby birds too, I believe, but I can't help loving them, they are so elegant and I even like their silly chattering. I'd be sorry if they didn't nest here anymore, my *elsters*."

Gertrude soon recovered from her unwanted holiday, but as her pregnancy increased she stayed more and more at home. She entertained a little but could hardly bring herself to visit her friends' houses and now on Saturday evening it was only Bernard who came to the shop. It was the same with theatres and films. They had been so fond of their almost weekly visits, but now Bernard had to go alone or take Charlotte or me instead. Gertrude was quite happy to stay at home and look after Marlinchen while I went to these entertainments with her husband. I hadn't been anywhere for over three years and for me it was wonderful to go to the theatre and read the reviews and choose the plays I'd like to see. I'd discuss my choice with Bernard and if he thought it a bad one he'd most likely talk me out of it. The concerts I left for Charlotte because I knew little about music and even Bernard, who loved imparting knowledge, couldn't face my ignorance.

The shop continued to do well and with the extra commission I earned I bought a really good dress for special occasions—and there were plenty of them those days. I also bought a pair of soft and delicate shoes for nearly forty pounds. It seemed a fortune to me, but they were worth a fortune because they were so comfortable and pretty. Occasionally I went to a hairdresser, just for the cutting really, but they insisted on doing other things and sometimes when I got home I put my expensive head under the tap, particularly if Bernard was taking me to the theatre. He'd say, "My God, what have you done to your hair?" and I'd feel so self-conscious I couldn't enjoy the play. The men who came to the shop liked it, though, and often asked me out; but except for the odd pub lunch I never accepted. Actually the dealers became a bit of a problem because they started to hang about the shop, sometimes even interfering when I was serving a customer. They thought they were being helpful, but I wished they'd go away. It wasn't only the improvement in my appearance that made me more attractive, it was my happiness and a new assurance that I'd never had before. It was so surprising to wake up in the mornings to all this happiness and interest in life.

There was one shadow that I kept in the back of my mind as much as possible, and that was my mother. To me she was almost like the wicked fairy, poor woman. She wasn't exactly a problem. She made no attempt to encroach on my life; she appeared to be reasonably content with her own. I used to feel a great bitterness towards her, but that had almost gone and it was mostly pity I felt now. Pity mixed with fear.

One afternoon when I was rearranging the shop window I noticed a nasty little dark blue car drawn up opposite the shop and there was Mr. Crimony slamming a grey felt hat on his head and helping mother out of the car. He carefully locked the doors and crossed the road holding her arm in a possessive manner. By this time I had reached the shop door and turned the notice that said "Open" to "Closed" and stood waiting for them to enter.

"Well, here we are," mother said nervously. "I must say it is a pretty little shop. Better than I expected, but very small. Do people really buy this kind of junk?"

Mr. Crimony took off his wide-brimmed grey felt hat. It was greasy, with a black band, and strangely repellent. He placed it on a plaster bust of Beethoven, slightly tilted it and said, "Of course they do. Antiques, that's what they are. My auntie had this kind of thing in her old cottage but we threw it out after she died. Rubbish it seemed to us, but it was worth a small fortune, we heard afterwards. A brass bed, I remember, and a slippery horsehair sofa, and things under glass domes, china and that. There was a square piano that looked for all the world like a coffin on tressels and some stuffed fish her Dad had caught years ago."

Mr. Crimony was waving his large arm about in a dangerous way so I hustled them into the back room and mother's mouth went down when she saw that I cooked, ate and sat in the same room. "Is this all you have, then?" she asked as I lit the gas under the kettle.

"No, there are two perfectly good rooms upstairs but it is more convenient to stay near the shop. Anyway, I like this room."

Mr. Crimony, who was trying hard to be pleasant, looked round and said, "That's a fine dresser you have there, Bella, and those plates are very handsome. Annie, have you noticed the dresser?"

Mother brightened: "Yes, some very nice things mixed in with the rubbish, but of course it's her trade." Then to me, "I must say it's very cosy in here," and she looked comfortable and at home sitting there in a Victorian buttoned chair waiting for her long-lost daughter to give her a cup of tea.

I didn't want to shatter the peace, there had so seldom been any between us, but I felt the time had come when I must tell her about Tommy Marline. I would have to fetch her from nursery school soon. Mother put down her tea cup and said in a relaxed way, "Pretty, isn't it? Hand-painted, I suppose." Then, looking at the twisted staircase that led upstairs, added, "I'd rather like to see the rest of the place while I'm here. If it's convenient, of course."

So I led her upstairs and first we went into the room that I used as a bedsitting-room. It had a good view of the Green with its chestnut trees and the scarlet buses flashing past half hidden by the bright young leaves. The room was really quite pretty now I'd redecorated it. The divan and recess where I hung my clothes were covered by Indian material, red and white with a design of peacocks, and there was a fine old writing table in the window where I did the shop's accounts, and a built-in bookcase and shelves for china, mostly Staffordshire. It was the most individual room I'd ever had and I asked brightly, "Do you like it, mother?"

She lifted the curtain covering my clothes: "So you've only got this place to hang your clothes. Why don't you get a wardrobe or something. You had a beautiful built-in one at home, remember? Mr. Crimony fits all his suits into it and with room to spare. I'm not saying it isn't a pretty room. You have made it very nice, considering, but I should do something about the wardrobe if I were you."

We went on to the little landing and I opened the door of the back room. It was filled with afternoon sun streaming on the little bed, the toys, the animals from the Noah's ark lying scattered on the floor and Big Teddy sitting in the now discarded high chair. The sun illuminated my baby's nursery as if it were a stage set.

My mother literally reeled. I've heard of people reeling from shock but never seen anyone do it before. She was tottering back on her heels and if I hadn't caught her, she would have fallen down the stairs. She pushed my supporting arms away and cried, "Charlie, come up here."

Charlie came stumbling up the narrow, twisting stairs, stumbling because his feet were too long to fit the treads. We retreated from the landing and he followed us into the sun-filled room. "Well, what's the matter?" he snapped. "Looks all right to me."

Mother clawed at him like a demented cat. "You fool, can't you see that this is a child's room? She's got a baby hidden away somewhere." She looked round wildly and made to pull the cot cover back.

Trying to control myself, I said in what I hoped was a calming voice: "Don't bother, your grand-daughter is in a nursery across the Green. Actually it is just about time to fetch her now. How about coming with me? It will only take a few minutes."

I held out my hand to her, hoping she would take it, but she slapped it and then my face and shouted, "You fool, at least you could have had an abortion! No wonder you have been in hiding all this time. Charlie, take me home."

She tottered down the stairs with poor Charlie stumbling after her. From an upstairs window I watched them scramble into their ugly little car and drive away, then I fetched Tommy home. Her hands were filled with paper butterflies they had been making in the nursery.

7

I DIDN'T see the Forbeses that weekend. I didn't see anyone except the customers who came to the shop—oh, and Miss Murray, but I couldn't really talk to her. She was quite pleasant the few times she had seen Tommy but she obviously didn't want to be involved with her in any way. She appeared to be afraid of being roped in for baby-sitting and that kind of thing, although she was the last person one could ask. She would have had a fit if a child upset a mug of milk on the carpet, or worse, if it did not make it clear that it needed to use its pot. Miss Murray was far kinder than she appeared to be but you couldn't confide in her or tell her the things your mother said and did.

Then Mr. Crimony came again and as usual without warning. I saw him from the window getting out of his horrible little car but he didn't open the door to mother because she wasn't there. He tapped on the shop window with something metal, a nail file I thought, but it turned out to be his car keys. I'd already locked the door and turned the cardboard notice to "Closed," but he went on tapping and eventually it so got on my nerves I let him in.

"Shall we go into the back room?" he said in a funereal voice. "I see you are closed," and I realized that to him the sign was very important, like KEEP OFF THE GRASS or something. It was nothing to me because I often changed the notice and there was one that said BACK IN TEN MINUTES that I used quite a lot.

We entered the back room which was dark that day although it was almost summer; the handsome plates on the dresser hardly noticed. Mr. Crimony went to sit on the buttoned Victorian chair, then changed it for an uncomfortable Gothic one already sold and waiting to be collected. He laid his hat, a bowler this time, and soiled driving gloves on the table and said heavily, "Bella, you may be wondering why I'm here. I can understand that you don't want to see me after the way your poor mother went on. But it was a shock, a fearful shock to us both, particularly to your mother, to hear that you had a child that no one knew about. A little girl, did you say it was? And what about her father? You're not married, are you?" I shook my head and he added, "No, we didn't think so."

He went on asking impertinent questions which I occasionally answered with a movement of my head. He was behaving as if he were a relation or someone in authority and after about ten minutes of this questioning I told him so and added, "If mother wants to know anything about my child, she can ask me herself."

He turned down his bottom lip and said darkly, "That's one thing she won't do. You don't know your own history, girl. I've known your mother for nearly forty years. Our parents were friends, particularly our fathers. Did you know that your grandfather was a coal merchant at one time, the same as my father was? Then he changed and became a timber merchant, in Pimlico of all places, and we didn't see so much of him. We still went for holidays together and I remember your mother, Annie, scrambling up the rocks and climbing cliffs, quite fearless she was and she swam well too. She was seven years younger than me and made me feel so ashamed. Then she could speak French. She'd picked it up from her mother, who was half French as you know, and because I was jealous I teased her quite a lot. So we quarrelled. She had a very quick temper, even in those days."

He stopped talking and lit a cigarette although he wasn't a smoking man and hadn't even a match in his pocket. I had silently handed him the box from the cooker. I couldn't speak because I was quietly praying over and over again, "Please God, don't let Crimony be my father."

He went rambling on. "After your grandfather died and left your family very badly off (we always said he'd have done better to stick to coal—wood wasn't his line), well they drifted back to Kilburn and managed somehow. Your uncle Ted got quite a nice little job in insurance and your mother became a pupil-teacher at the school where she stayed all those years. Games and French were her subjects and I think at first she quite enjoyed herself there. She was very keen on tennis in those days and used to play on some courts at Swiss Cottage. Sometimes I used to join her there on a Saturday afternoon but I wasn't in her class. The man who owned the courts used to coach her quite a bit and didn't charge a penny. Thought he'd make her a champion, no less."

I stopped praying for a moment and said, "It's strange she never let me play, I wanted to at school and it might have got my weight down a bit."

Mr. Crimony fixed his pale blue eyes on me in such a way that we were staring each other out: "It's not surprising that she didn't want you to take up tennis, because you were the reason she had to give it up. Annie was very bitter about that, very bitter."

I said, "Now I come to think about it, tennis champions don't seem to go in for babies much, not like actresses. If she felt like that about it, why did she get married?"

Crimony's pale eyes held mine even more intently and I thought, "Now it's coming."

He hunched his shoulders and growled like a bad-tempered old dog. "This is going to be a shock to you. You were conceived out of wedlock. Your mother, who I'd hoped to marry, had behaved like any slut of the streets and had had intercourse with a man she hardly knew, a man she met playing tennis. It took her four months to persuade him to marry her, four months of purgatory. Her brother Ted knocked him to the ground, but that didn't help much. You see, his family were against it, didn't think Annie good enough. They gave in eventually and there was a quiet wedding, in a registry office I believe. I didn't go, of course. I didn't see Annie again for at least six years and I was married by then myself."

I was saying under my breath, "Thank you, God, thank you that I'm not Crimony's child," and when I finished thanking God I started to laugh, I couldn't stop. It wasn't a happy laugh, but I felt better for it, and looking at Mr. Crimony sitting in his Gothic chair I could see he was shaking with a kind of laughter—or perhaps tears. I was longing to get him out of the house so that I could think about my parents, so many things were becoming clear. I opened my mouth to say, "You had better go now, Mr. Crimony," but instead I said, "Perhaps you'd like a drink before you go, Mr. Crimony. There's some sherry on the dresser," and I fetched two glasses from the shop.

8

ON THE first Monday of May Gertrude telephoned and asked me to close "the silly old shop" and spend the day with her, gardening. "You haven't been here the last two weekends and you can't imagine what is happening out there in the garden. The flowers seem to be completely taking over, every root, bulb or seed I have planted has taken root and the place is like a jungle."

"But what about the gardener I sometimes see mowing the lawns?" I asked.

"Well, that's just it. He only does the mowing, pruning and general tidying up, but has no contact with the flowers, that's my job. I love it normally."

I remembered her condition and agreed to come although there were several things I'd planned to do in the shop. It was a perfect early summer day, ideal for gardening, and after what I'd been through with Crimony I needed a change. So I hung "Closed" on the door and set off for Richmond by bus because Bernard wouldn't allow Gertrude to drive now she was five months pregnant and the baby had started to flutter about. He seemed to think a moving baby was more vulnerable.

Gertrude was waiting for me in the courtyard at the front of the house. She was examining a passion flower cutting that she had recently planted hoping it would climb up the walls of the house. It had been about three feet high when I'd last seen it but now it was careering up the wall and had already reached a bedroom window. I laughed and said she was like Jack and the beanstalk. She pointed out a patch of wild violets. "You remember the violet I dug up from the roadside—look how it has multiplied. Even the carved bear has canary-creeper growing over his back. I don't know where it came from, but I haven't the heart to pull it up. Soon it will be a golden lion."

We walked through the cool house into the garden, blazing with sun and colour, a jumble of tulips mixed with forget-me-nots and groups of heavy-smelling hyacinths, borders of polyanthus and the luxuriant leaves of peonies springing up and hiding struggling small plants. Against a crumbling stone wall there was a patch of blood-red wallflowers. I have never cared for wallflowers much except for their scent; to me they seem rather shaggy and shapeless, but these were perfect, like an illustration in a gardening book. We went to the little potting-shed/conservatory where Gertrude started her seeds in boxes and pots. It must have been five weeks ago that I had helped her plant the annuals intended to fill the summer beds and the stone urns she was so fond of. The glass had been removed and green leaves were pouring out of the boxes, the petunias and dahlias already in bud and demanding to be transplanted.

There were a few boxes at the end of the row where the green wasn't very high and Gertrude remarked, "That's queer, these are weeks behind the others and I remember they were all planted at the same time. It was a Sunday and you helped me."

I said, with shame, "Those are the ones I planted."

We both started to laugh and Gertrude, still laughing, said, "That proves Bernard is right as usual. He says that primitive people believe that pregnant women have special powers and they use them to plant the crops. Rather hard on the pregnant women, though."

We planted, thinned out the hardy annuals, cut back and weeded, filled the urns with young petunias and trailing lobelia and watered the transplanted seedlings. There were so many surplus young plants Gertrude insisted that I take them home and plant them in the yard attached to the house. Although it had a certain amount of sun and was fairly private I'd never considered it as a garden, but, now I thought about it, I remembered noticing some green leaves pushing up through the tired earth that could be Michaelmas daisies and also some golden rod, and there was a straggling rose bush that had gone wild and a clump of something that might be self-seeded hollyhocks. On my way home I bought a garden fork and I started my garden that evening.

It was enclosed with high walls on two sides, a fence with a few lilac bushes above on the west side and on the south a low wall and large gates that led to the main road and were never opened. The ground was partly paved and partly wild green weeds which I gradually turned into a rough lawn. There were slight indications that someone had once made a herbaceous bed round three sides of the yard but more recently coke had been stored there. As I dug up splinters of glass, chips of china and coke I pretended to myself that it was a suitable place to find small treasure, so I dug deeper than I would have normally. I did find a few small coins, a cut-glass salt-cellar with an almost undamaged silver top, and something that might have been the remains of an antique bracelet but was more likely part of an old copper pipe. But my deep digging was rewarded when I exposed some really large York stones which I made into a low wall with climbing flowers planted both sides. If it had been higher I'd have planted wisteria there; instead I had it growing up the south wall of the cottage, dark mauve, and with it the rare white floribunda called "Alba," and I hope they are still growing there to this day. The soil was tainted and dead, just dirt really, so I bought expensive earth and put it round each plant and sprinkled bone meal over the entire garden. After I bought a hose for watering I promised myself that it was the last thing I'd buy until the autumn. Then I broke my promise and spent ten pounds on a magnolia tree and this made me feel really ashamed and for the rest of the summer the only thing I spent on the garden was my time.

Almost every evening we gardened, Tommy and I. I let her stay until the dusk came and sometimes so late we went to bed at the same time. She so enjoyed stirring up the earth and watering the flowers with her little can, often getting so wet I had to take her soaking clothes off and, if it was still warm, I let her play naked. Fortunately no interfering neighbours could see us. She liked to run round the garden with her arms behind her and the palms of her hands facing upwards so that she almost appeared to be flying in the pallid evening light.

One evening when the watering was finished we were eating a simple meal of milk, cornflakes and fruit, sitting at the garden table I'd bought from a junk shop and painted white. We were eating by the light thrown into the garden from the cottage windows, but parts of the garden were almost dark. Suddenly we were disturbed by a rattling at the gate, then there was a head jumping up and down like something to be shot at at a fair. Perhaps it said something above the sound of the traffic, but I wasn't sure.

Leaving our unfinished meal, I hurried Tommy into the house and through the side door that lead to the shop and, when I switched on the light, there was a face against the window, peering. It seemed a mad face to me, but when it started calling "Bella, Bella" the voice was vaguely familiar. Then, to my dismay, I saw it was Stephen, not looking mad at all, just annoyed at not being recognized. Reluctantly I let him into the shop and then into the back room and said crossly, "I wish people would leave me alone. I suppose mother gave you my address."

I don't think he heard me because he was too intent on staring at Tommy, who had picked up a toy trumpet and was handing it to him to blow. He turned away from her and said in a cruel voice, "Is this the child your mother thinks is mine? She must be mad. You said you were pregnant by me as an excuse not to share the insurance money. Don't think it is the money I care about, keep it for all I care, but the deceit, trying to pass that little blackamoor off as my child."

I shouted, "Shut up, you conceited idiot. I never passed her off as your child, she's mine. I don't even know her father's name, so she's doubly mine. Mother has never seen her and didn't even know she existed until a couple of weeks ago, so what right has she to interfere?" And I scooped my child up in my arms as if to protect her.

For a moment she looked as if she were about to cry. I don't think she had ever heard angry voices before. She buried her face in my neck, then looked out and with the sweetest smile again held the trumpet out to Stephen. To my surprise he gently took it and blew a

long note and as the smile broadened he blew another. My anger
faded. It seemed ridiculous to shout at a man blowing a tin trumpet.
I put Tommy down and drew the curtains as if it were an ordinary
evening. Anger and fear had left the room and I said, "I was just about
to make a cup of coffee. Would you like one, Stephen?"

I put Tommy to bed and we sat talking in a friendly way. I asked
after old friends I hadn't seen for years and he told me of marriages
that had ended and of new ones that had taken place, jobs that ended
and new ones that hadn't always taken place. Stephen was fortunate
and still had his advertising job. Then we became more personal and
he told me about his girlfriends, several casual ones and three more
permanent, that is to say they had lived in the flat we used to share.
I'd always felt like a lodger when I lived there. It had never been a
home like the shop was. Everything had to be done Stephen's way
and my belongings tucked away and not in evidence. I supposed it
had been the same for his other girlfriends. Poor things, no wonder
they didn't last long. Then he was asking me questions and of course
the main one was my daughter's parentage. Who was her father? I
told him the simple truth but he could hardly believe it because it
sounded so unlike my usual behaviour. He didn't understand that
when one is unhappy and without hope one does strange things,
perhaps even murder. He went on asking unnecessary questions: "But
what did he look like? Was he very dark? What did he do for a living?"

All I remembered was that he was kind, that he appeared to have
problems, though I couldn't remember what they were, and that he
wore this rather smelly red velvet jacket, and even went to bed in it.

"He doesn't sound very attractive to me," Stephen said, staring
hard at my face. "You could do better than that," and he ran his
finger down my scarred face. "This thing has improved so much one
hardly notices it after a few minutes."

I felt my hand instinctively rising towards my scar but it didn't
reach it and I said offhandedly, "People get used to it and so have I."
I knew his next question would be, Had I a lover? He might even
suggest that we become lovers again. I didn't want him as a lover; but
I needed friends. I had so few.

9

So stephen became my friend, not a trusted friend, but a friend. He used to arrive without warning, sometimes with a bottle of wine and sometimes without, but he usually expected a meal. He came about once a week, often when it was fine because now the days were drawing out; he liked to sit in the garden if it was warm enough. He even fixed an outdoor light and gave me two garden chairs, and the gritty old backyard turned into a flower-filled patio with whitewashed walls. Sometimes Tommy was still running around when Stephen came. At first he was uneasy with her, but when she talked to him in her trusting way and put her small brown hand on his knee and called him "Friend," he was won over. She called him "Friend" because I'd told her he was a friend when they first met.

One evening he took us both to Richmond Park to see the deer, and when he heard the passers-by remarking how beautiful Tommy was, he became quite proud, as if he really were her father. Another evening he took us to visit friends of his living at Kew, a photographer and his wife. They were delighted with Tommy and took photographs of her eating and playing. They thought she would do well as a child model; but I wasn't at all keen on the idea because it would upset her settled life between the shop and nursery, just when things were going so well and we didn't need the money.

I wanted to keep the Forbeses apart from Stephen and seldom mentioned them to each other; but he soon discovered that we were often away at weekends and that I went to the theatre now and then. One Saturday evening, when Bernard was helping me to close the shop, Stephen arrived, his golden hair glittering in the evening sun as he crossed the road. He said he happened to be passing, but I knew he was just being inquisitive or even spying for my mother. Of course I had to introduce them, particularly as Tommy ran up to him and flung her arms round his legs and called him "Friend" so it was obvious he was a frequent caller. It amused me to see the two men summing each other up.

Bernard seemed a little huffed. He hung the "Closed" notice on the door and said, "I'm afraid we are about to leave. My wife is waiting for us at home and we're late already."

I said, "Yes, we'd better go out by the side door now it's all locked up. I'm sorry we have to rush off like this, Stephen."

"It doesn't matter," he said petulantly. "As I said, I was just passing."

We all left together but I had to run back to collect a plastic bag containing our things for the weekend and to turn the water heater off—I always forget things if I'm rushed. When I rejoined the men I saw that by a coincidence they had parked their cars nose to tail against the Green, Stephen's an MG and Bernard's a large Volvo he used for work. They were talking cars and seemed more relaxed and Bernard was holding Tommy in his arms ready to put her in her own little seat at the back.

We parted in a friendly way but immediately we left the Green behind, Bernard was asking me questions: "So that's the man you left home for," he said teasingly. "He's certainly handsome, except that his eyes are slightly close together. Didn't you say he was a little on the mean side?"

Feeling rather disloyal to Stephen I agreed, but added, "He isn't as bad as he used to be. He brings me wine quite often and he gave me the garden chairs and fixed the light, you know, so he must have improved. I expect I didn't know how to manage him."

"And now you do?" he asked smiling.

I thought for a moment. Did I know how to manage him? "No, not really, but I don't care for him all that much. I used to be fearfully vulnerable when I did."

We crossed the bridge and weaved our way through Richmond's

narrow streets towards the Forbeses' house. When we reached it and I stepped into their courtyard I felt I was on enchanted ground. I think my daughter felt the same and she always called it home.

It was May. Hardly anyone noticed Gertrude was pregnant except that she had this radiance and just to look at her made one feel happy and at peace. Bernard adored her more than ever and kept saying, "Look at her, isn't she lovely?" When we were alone, he'd sometimes become quite apprehensive and ask me if I thought thirty-seven was too old to have a first baby. "You don't think anything could go wrong, do you?" he'd say in a most unBernard-like way. "The doctor would tell me if anything was wrong. I asked him about all the gardening she did and walking the dog in the park, but he said pregnancy wasn't an illness, exercise was good for her."

That weekend they teased me a little about Stephen, but it was kind teasing and I didn't mind. I wasn't very pleased, though, when they got on to the subject of my mother. They really pitied her. Poor woman, deprived of her lovely little grand-daughter and living in Kilburn with the horrible Mr. Crimony smelling of coal-dust. I said she was happy as she was; she liked her work in the travel agency and seemed to like Mr. Crimony too. She'd known him most of her life and if she wanted to see her grandchild she was welcome to come any day she liked. That wasn't quite true; I was dreading her coming.

Fortunately they soon forgot about my mother because some German friends arrived with a small boy not much older than Marlinchen and they played together very well as soon as we left them to their own devices, which consisted of mildly teasing the old dog, putting stones on the swing and picking wild flowers in Gertrude's thicket. They left the flowers scattered on the kitchen floor and when she saw them Gertrude was upset because they had brought may into the house. She kept saying, "It's fearfully unlucky to bring may into the house. Don't tell Bernard."

I tried to reassure her by saying that may in the house was considered lucky in some countries; but she looked at me with her great eyes filled with disbelief and said, "We are not in other countries, we're in England."

She still appeared uneasy when it was time for Bernard to drive me home. As we said goodbye, I whispered in her ear, "I don't think it was may. It looked like blackthorn to me and I definitely saw a thorn."

It was worthwhile lying to see the relief on her face as she murmured thoughtfully, "It's late for blackthorn, but it's shady down there in the thicket. Yes, it could easily have been blackthorn."

It was as if a ripple of our talk about mother had touched her because she telephoned the following evening, when calls are cheap, and said that she had run into Stephen, which must have taken quite a lot of arranging because he lived in Chelsea and she hardly ever left Kilburn. She said, "I asked Stephen about your little girl and he said that she was a lovely child but he wasn't her father. Is this true, that he isn't her father?"

I told her that it was true; Stephen wasn't Marline's father and that I'd never said that he was. Actually her father was "a foreign gentleman" who had returned to his country.

"A foreign gentleman, but what kind of a father is that?" she shrilled.

"Don't do that, mother," I said. "You're spitting."

"Spitting! How can you tell if I'm spitting or not, you stupid girl? What about this foreigner? Is he paying for his daughter, I'd like to know."

I told her that he knew nothing about his daughter. She'd been born months after he left the country. As for money, we were managing very well and didn't need any. I was even saving.

There was silence for a moment and I could almost hear mother making an effort, then, "I must come and see this grandchild of mine. I'll let you know when. Oh, and what kind of foreigner is the child's father? Where does he come from?"

I hesitated, then said, "Brazilian." I knew there were a lot of very dark people in Brazil.

I hated lies and now I'd been forced to tell them two days running. When I tell lies I can feel my eyes flicking like a hen's. It does not matter on the telephone, but it is a tiresome habit when one is face to face with a friend who would be happier not knowing the truth. Flicking eyes immediately make them suspicious. I can look them in the face when I lie but it's the flicking eyes that give me away.

The first few days of June were very hot and the white petals from the chestnut trees on the Green fell to the grass like melting snow. At lunchtime young men lay on the grass without shirts as if it were a beach and mothers with young children in striped pushchairs sat under the trees while the elderly stiffly arranged themselves on the benches. All day the dedicated dog-lovers circled round, attached to their dogs by leads. Sometimes they were set free and a ball was thrown for their entertainment. At one end of the Green there was a much-used cricket pavilion and at the other a less-used public convenience— a good one people said—catering for men, women and invalids.

I watched these things from the shop window. It faced south and the sun came shimmering in, robbing the antiques of their mystery. In the harsh light every blemish was accentuated, the life went from the paintings, carved gilt looked tawdry and the antique furniture was heavily scored with cracks and marks and appeared more second-hand than antique. Recently I had cleaned the glass domes with some patent stuff to make them sparkle; but now I could see they were all marked with greasy streaks and the shop window was the same. I spent most of the day polishing. Fortunately there were few customers and I was able to work in peace—until a bright blue MG drew up on the other side of the road and out stepped Stephen and a long-legged girl, rather a beautiful golden girl. I watched them darting through the heavy traffic. At certain times it was controlled by a lollipop man, but this wasn't one of them. They came into the shop with happy smiles on their handsome faces and there were introductions. Miss Longlegs was an American actress called Brit Bonner who had a small part in a new musical, so Stephen said. They had met at a publicity party only seven days ago and had seen each other every day since, so they were like old friends in a way. They chattered like excited birds, laughing and contradicting each other. I'd never seen Stephen so gay, more like a boy than a rather mean man of thirty years.

I closed the shop and we had tea in the garden, an early tea because Brit had to appear at the theatre. She told me that it was the first time she had acted in the West End or in any large theatre. Stephen said, "Show Bella your cuttings, pet," and out of her large handbag she produced some crumpled reviews of shows she had appeared in at small theatres in the States with favourable mentions of herself: "Miss Bonner is a bombshell" or "Brit Bonner is an interesting newcomer," and the more exciting "Beautiful Brit Bonner cracks the whip."

I went through the motions of being impressed but as she returned the cuttings to her handbag she said wistfully, "I really want to be a serious actress, but have to take the parts I'm offered. I began by being the maid or even worse, the ASM." She asked to be shown over the cottage and Stephen rushed her round as if the place belonged to him and she was saying, "Fantastic, fantastic," all the time. Wherever she went she left a faint but haunting scent. In the garden I'd hoped it was my flowers but when I followed Brit into the house I knew it was her smelling so expensive. When they left the smell still lingered.

10

ONE MORNING when I was returning from taking Tommy to the nursery I could hear the telephone ringing away from the other side of the road, so I dived in between the streaming cars, to the great annoyance of the lollipop man, who was waving his pole at me. By the time I had opened the shop door and seized the instrument it was giving a feeble last ring; but I'd caught it in time and Gertrude's voice floated down the line. She wanted to tell me about a strange dream she had had; she seemed quite obsessed by it. In the dream she was walking on marble floors among tall pillars. Sometimes she was walking under a roof and at other times there was only the intense blue sky above, but always the pillars and in the distance white buildings. She was wearing simple, rather roughly-made sandals on her feet, but her dress was a kind of robe made of finely woven material, very pleasant to touch. She could still remember the feel of it between her fingers. She said she was searching for someone. It could have been Bernard, but at the time she had thought it unlikely because the dream was taking place two thousand years ago. I asked how she knew. Did she have a calendar?

"No, nothing like that," she said vaguely. "But I just knew it was two thousand years ago. There was no sign of the 1980s anywhere. I sat on a marble bench that had been warmed by the sun and watched a little figure in the distance walking towards me and growing larger and larger and then I saw he had a large scroll under his arm that could have been a rolled painting and I thought that after all it really was Bernard I was searching for. I cried, 'Bernard!' very loud and he answered, 'Gertrude, hush,' and we were in our bed at home together."

I said, "Yes, it was a strange dream, but rather lovely."

"Lovely in a way but extraordinary too. You see, Bernard was dreaming almost the same dream at the same time. He *was* the figure in the distance carrying the scroll, which was quite heavy, and he never got close to me although he could see me sitting amongst the pillars in the distance. I asked him if he was wearing robes or an ordinary suit. 'Oh, robes, of course,' he said. Actually he'd thought he must be Julius Caesar until he saw me sitting on my marble bench. Then his one idea was to reach me, but however hard he walked, we were always apart. It was as if the ground were slipping beneath his feet, almost a nightmare really. What do you think it means? Have you ever heard of people sharing a dream like that?"

"Well," I said thoughtfully, "I don't think I have. But you and Bernard are so close, much closer than most married people. You may have had another life together two thousand years ago."

She was quiet for almost a minute, then said, "Yes, you could be right. Bernard and I may have lived together two thousand years ago and even at other times too. It is certainly very weird. The dream was beautiful in a way and I'll never forget it, but I wouldn't like to share dreams every night. Would you?"

"No," I said, "but it couldn't happen to me. I've no one to share my dreams with."

I replaced the receiver because someone was entering the shop. Then I saw it was Miss Murray, all dressed for summer in a pure silk dress with a matching cape to hide her curved back. She was carrying a basket containing slightly damaged china she thought I might care to buy cheaply. "I can put up with the rivets, it's cracks I can't stand— and as for chips, they really disgust me. Look at this Rockingham poodle with a nasty little chip on his blue cushion and this Minton jug quite ruined by a chip on its lip, and as for cracks, look at that," and she held out a Crown Derby dish. It had a minute crack on its rim and some of the gold had been washed away—with strong detergents most likely. "You can have that for nothing. I can't bear the sight of it."

She emptied her basket and asked if I'd seen anything of the

Forbeses lately. It was some time since they had visited her shop and she had some heavy gilt frames that might interest them. I told her about their shared dream, but she was sceptical and put it down to pregnant fancies. "Women get very strange at these times, you know. They are not normal at all."

I said I supposed so, although I didn't agree. I was convinced that Gertrude and Bernard's dream was something very special that could only happen to people who were as close as they were. All the day their dream kept creeping into my mind and it was as if I'd shared in it as well.

Now July had come I'd sit in my walled garden listening to cricket being played on the Green—the crack of the ball being hit and sometimes a gentle clapping—and, when the stream of heavy traffic thinned, pigeons could be heard cooing. I was usually alone after Tommy went to bed. Stephen seldom came to see us now he had Brit and, when he did, he talked about nothing but her and his fear that the musical was coming to an end, already empty seats were casting shadows on his happiness. He'd ask me what he was to do if Brit returned to America. He had already asked her to marry him but she couldn't make up her mind. Not that she didn't love him, only for the time being she felt she must put her career first; later on, when she was more established, things would be different, and so on. I'd say more or less what he wanted me to say, agreeing that she was beautiful and tremendously talented, that she obviously loved him very much and that it was likely she would be offered good parts in West End theatres, although I knew little about the theatre world and had only met Brit once. At least I did know she was beautiful and seemed to be in love with Stephen, so I could talk convincingly about that. I really liked what I'd seen of the girl, but it was boring sitting out there in the dusk talking about her non-stop. The tobacco plants were smelling so lovely too. I didn't really care for Stephen any more. All the same we were friends and I would have liked him to take a little interest in me and my life as he did before Brit came. It wasn't quite so boring when he brought wine.

Saturdays were more of a problem than they used to be because

Tommy wasn't content to play with odds and ends in the shop. She fretted to be in the garden and wanted to drag all her toys out of the toy box. One afternoon there was a fearful acid smell of burning coming from the kitchen and I remembered I'd left a pie in the oven. I left a trusted customer in charge of the shop and hurried to the kitchen to save my pie only it wasn't a pie burning in the oven but a plastic toy piano and ten little men Tommy must have put there. I took them out and held them under the running tap although the piano would never play again and the men looked as if they had been hit by an atom bomb, their faces all warped and their limbs twisted.

I think it was the same Saturday Tommy roasted her toy piano that Mother at last appeared to inspect her grand-child. I remember that as soon as she opened the shop door she shouted above the ring of the bell, "What a strange smell! I don't like it at all." There stood mother with her darting eyes and Mr. Crimony, with a nervous half-smile on his face, standing behind her.

I was serving a rather valued customer at the time, but she said she would come again and melted away like a snowflake leaving me there with my hands filled with Victorian door handles all decorated with hand-painted flowers. I awkwardly held them out to mother and said, "Pretty, aren't they?"

But her eyes were fixed on Tommy and she never glanced at the door handles. "So this is the daughter of a foreign gentleman," she said bitterly. "Mr. Crimony, just take a look at this child. How could she be related to me in any way."

Tommy, who had been watching the children and dogs playing on the Green, left the window and ran up to Mr. Crimony and, laughing, snatched his repellent hat away from his hand and put it on her own head, then danced round the shop singing to herself.

He watched her for a moment and said soothingly, "No, I can't say she takes after you in any way, but she's a nice little girl and takes after her dad I expect."

The hat dance finished. Tommy handed it back to Mr. Crimony and stood beside him looking at his face hopefully. He fumbled in his pockets but all he could find was a cough drop. "See how she's making up to you, sly little creature. Well, one thing's for certain, she's never coming to my house."

I said coldly, "Don't worry, mother, I have no intention of taking her to your unhappy house. There's no love there, only bitterness."

I replaced the door handles in the window and hung the notice "Closed" on the door and calmly asked mother if she were staying for tea. "I expect I'll be accused of bitterness if I don't," she said ungraciously, looking at Tommy all the time and pretending she wasn't. Then in an unnatural voice she called the child to her and Tommy, looking for reassurance, slowly walked towards her. "So you're Tommy Marline," Mother barked and, not knowing what to do next, she took her right hand and shook it, which made Tommy laugh.

"I'm Marlinchen in my home over there," and she pointed to nowhere in particular.

"Now Tommy or Marline or whoever you are, I've brought you a little present. Two presents in fact," and mother fumbled about in her bag and produced a small, rather pretty doll wearing a hat, and a mechanical clown who somersaulted about the carpet. Tommy was delighted with her presents and mother said quite cheerfully, "They are better than a silly old cough drop, aren't they?"

Mr. Crimony, looking quite sad, said, "But you didn't tell me we were bringing presents. I'd have brought the little girl something if I'd known. What would you like me to bring the next time I come, Tommy?"

And without hesitation she answered, "A violin," which was strange because I didn't know if she had ever seen one.

We sat in the kitchen eating a family tea, Mr. Crimony stuffing away on an iced lemon cake I'd made for Gertrude and mother asking questions: Had I seen Stephen lately? and that kind of thing, speaking to me but looking at her grandchild. She said, "I would have quite enjoyed a grandchild if it had been a normal one but illegitimacy combined with colour is too much for me. It's unnatural."

"Hardly that, mother," I said. "I'm sorry but I must clear away now because we're going away for the weekend."

Mother jumped to her feet and snapped, "Get on with it, then, we won't detain you."

At that moment Tommy, who had very sharp ears, suddenly shouted, "Bernard's here," and darted to the shop door, returning a minute later in Bernard's arms.

I was hardly in a state for introductions so he introduced himself and told mother how much he had wanted to meet her. Then he turned to Mr. Crimony and said in a very friendly way, "You're in coal, aren't you? Bella tells me she worked for you at one time, her first job, wasn't it?"

Mother interrupted, "Yes, and a very nice job too, but she threw it away and went in for antiques. She would have done well if she'd stayed, wouldn't she, Mr. Crimony?"

He looked doubtful. "I don't think she would have if she didn't like the work. She tried, mind you, but she never seemed interested in coal. No, she's better as she is."

Bernard agreed, then asked if he could drive them home to Kilburn. "You see I know where you live," he said reassuringly.

Mother declined. "We came by car," she said grandly. "We wouldn't attempt a complicated journey like this by public transport."

Within a few minutes they had left the house. Mr. Crimony had kissed Tommy goodbye but mother had only patted her on the head exclaiming, "Gracious! her hair feels as woolly as it looks!"

We watched them drive away from the shop window and Bernard put his arm round me for a moment and said, "My dear, it wasn't too bad, was it? Your mother was a bit difficult, but old Crimony isn't so bad and I didn't smell the coal dust you mentioned."

I gave a shaky laugh. "He may not smell of coal dust any more, all the same I don't want him as a stepfather. Perhaps it won't happen after all these years. It's a strange relationship they have."

11

IT WAS arranged that the shop was to be closed for the first two weeks in August while Tommy and I stayed with the Forbeses in Richmond. Gertrude's baby was due in late September, but already Bernard did not like her being more or less alone in the house all day. I felt that he was too apprehensive and encouraging disaster with all his fears. Why should Gertrude, who had been up and down the stairs thousands of times, suddenly take to falling down them? She was no longer allowed to take her aged and gentle greyhound for walks, driving the car was forbidden and also household shopping without a companion. Gardening was frowned upon too, so the gardener put in far more hours than he used to. "It's such a bore having the little man around so much," she complained. "At least he never puts a foot in my thicket. He's really a spy, you know. If I bend down to cut off a few dead flower heads, he tells Bernard. Now you are here perhaps he will leave me alone." All Bernard's fussing had made me nervous too, particularly when she insisted on bathing Marline herself, lifting her in and out of the bath as if she were as light as a kitten.

Except for the air of apprehension creeping round the house it was a happy fortnight. The weather was good and we spent a lot of time in the luxuriant garden and ate picnic luncheons in the thicket under Gertrude's juniper tree. The clearing had been enlarged and there was a table to eat from, and urns containing red and yellow nasturtiums which had become almost wild and were climbing freely up the bushes and trees like flames. I called it the Burning Bush Restaurant. We ate such lovely things there—salads and French cheeses, smoked salmon and raspberries and cream, all my favourite things.

Sometimes we drank white wine and other times iced coffee. It was a very good restaurant indeed. Gertrude looked the picture of health, sitting there glowing against the background of flowers and intense greenery, rather like someone in a Rousseau painting, particularly when the magpies appeared amongst the leaves. One day she said in her dreamy way: "I've asked Bernard to scatter my ashes here when I die. You will remind him, won't you?"

I smiled and said I'd try to remember, but might be dead myself by then. "What about Bernard?" I asked teasingly. "Where will you scatter his ashes?"

She appeared quite startled: "Of course Bernard won't die before me! I couldn't live without him. I'd never manage. Even as a joke don't suggest such a thing."

She made me feel almost guilty and to change the subject I turned her attention to Marline, who had climbed a little way up the cherry tree, trying to reach the remaining withered fruit. We sat watching her, then Gertrude said: "You have been such a good mother under great difficulties. We often talk about it, Bernard and I. If anything happens to me you would look after my child, wouldn't you? There's no one I'd trust as well as you. I know I'm being morbid, but just say you will and we'll never mention it again."

I promised, although I felt afraid of such a responsibility, What did "looking after" exactly mean? Suppose I died, who would look after Tommy-Marline? Not my mother, I hoped.

We had no more morbid conversations and I'll always remember that two weeks' holiday as a very special time. There were no more visits to the theatre now because of leaving Gertrude alone, but almost every evening Bernard gave me a chess lesson, which I enjoyed although I found the game very difficult: my mind was too undisciplined and more suited for a game of drafts. Some evenings we sat listening to classical records, with the french windows open to the dusky garden, and music began to mean something to me. It was as if I'd been deaf before. When I went home I borrowed a stack of records to play on my inferior machine and my lonely evenings disappeared because the musicians became my dear friends. I hoped that one day Bernard would take me to a concert. I don't know why but I imagined they would be very formal affairs with everyone wearing evening dress, far grander than the theatre.

The shop was very quiet during the second half of August and I did little business. One afternoon Stephen arrived in a great state because the musical was about to close and Brit was considering returning to the States as she had had several attractive offers, one a straight part which appeared to be exactly what she so hoped for. She was determined to be a serious actress, not just a beautiful one, and couldn't afford to miss her chances. I advised Stephen to let her go and to follow a little later when she had settled down. He could combine a visit to America with his advertising work and it was quite likely that his firm would pay most of his expenses. On the other hand if things became desperate, he could live there more or less permanently.

I tried to reassure him with my trite suggestions, but he turned on me almost shouting, his voice was so angry: "So you want to get rid of me! You don't really care if I marry Brit or not or if you ever see me again for that matter. You only care about the pompous Bernard and his bloody Volvo 245."

It took me a moment to remember what a Volvo was: I've never been interested in cars. How clever of Stephen to know the car's number! I said, "Of course I care about Bernard and Gertrude, they are my special friends and so are you. I haven't many. To tell the truth, I've missed you a lot lately since you have been so occupied with Brit. I didn't resent it, but I missed you. It's not so bad now I have all these records to listen to. I play them most evenings."

"Records!" he said scornfully. "You speak like a child. I suppose Bernard is improving your tiny mind with music now."

I laughed and slipped my hand into his. "I think you've had a bit of a quarrel with Brit and are taking it out on me. Let's collect Tommy from the nursery and eat ice-cream together by the river. It's too early for a drink."

We called for Tommy and drove to Teddington Lock and, leaving the car outside The Anglers, crossed the blue and white footbridge to the tow path on the other side and walked towards Ham House. It wasn't long before we heard chimes playing a few bars from the Harry Lime theme and Tommy ran ahead to catch the ice-cream van, which was about to leave the river bank for the more profitable housing estate in the village. We sat by the river slowly licking our cornets and Stephen asked, "Do you think Bernard ever eats pink ice-cream on a public path?" I said he might if the chimes played Scarlatti, even then it was unlikely. We slowly walked back to The Anglers and collected the car. It was three weeks before we saw Stephen again. The next morning it was raining and Tommy was covered in midge bites.

But life wasn't all rain and midge bites. I bought some beautiful Georgian chairs from a private house that was being dismantled in a hurry. There were four of them and I brought them home in a taxi because I knew they would be snatched up immediately if I left them behind. I gave their delighted owner a cheque for the eighty pounds they asked and couldn't believe my luck. As far as I could see everything else in the house was almost worthless, but these chairs were part of a set divided between the family when their granny died. "Real mahogany they are. You don't often see chairs like that now; but we can't take them with us, we're going to Australia, you see."

As soon as I got home I telephoned Mary Meadows and she hurried round and we spent the evening cleaning and polishing them. Mary sold them on her stall the next day and we divided the profit between us, sixty pounds each. It was the best thing that had happened to me since I'd been in antiques, my first real success. After that Mary trusted me to buy for the shop, and sometimes on slack days I went to sales and bought from private houses as well. It made a pleasant change because occasionally I resented being confined to the shop for so many hours, particularly during the summer, seeing girls flashing past my windows in their pretty summer dresses and with the sun shining on their hair. In September my weekend visits to the Forbeses would cease for a time because Charlotte was coming to live in the house for at least a month and a nurse was expected. Gertrude had insisted on having her baby at home although the doctor was against it. She felt that a hospital was too impersonal a place for such a wanted and special baby. "This is just the right kind of house for one of those blue plaques. I know this child will grow up to be famous in some way, but perhaps most mothers think that. Anyway, famous or not, I won't have him born in a hospital."

We had our last picnic under the juniper tree, Gertrude ignoring the food I'd arranged on the table but almost greedily gulping down the last of the juniper berries that grew on the shady side of the tree—the berries so blue and poisonous-looking, and smelling strange too. I'd seen her do this before; but this time she was snatching at the fruit with her long white hands and putting several in her mouth at once, and her lips became stained and her dress all spattered with the needle-leaves. I wished Bernard were there to control her. Eventually I did get her to eat a little of the salmon mayonnaise, but her lips and indeed her dress were so stained with the juniper juice that she had a wild look. When Bernard came home I told him what had happened in the thicket. Although the stains had been removed I thought he should know in case she were taken ill during the night.

The gardener was told discreetly to destroy any berries that appeared on the tree, but we need not have worried because she stopped going to the thicket and we had no more picnics there. Sometimes she walked in her garden amongst the great dahlias with their brilliant fleshy flowers and wished she had not planted so many. "I'd no idea they would grow as large as this," she said and walked among the roses instead. She mostly kept to the house during her last month of pregnancy, often sitting by the open french windows reading seventeenth-century poetry. She was particularly fond of Marvell and Donne. In spite of her enlarged body, she looked extraordinarily beautiful sitting there with the greyhound lying at her feet. The dog was so quiet I often forgot she existed. I had never heard her bark, but sometimes on walks she would suddenly start running in ever-widening circles, and when she returned she had such a proud and happy face as if remembering old triumphs.

When Charlotte came to stay she took over most of the cooking and the food was not so imaginative, in fact there was an air of school dinners about it—steak and kidney pies that were not pies because the pastry had been cooked separately, nourishing but tasteless stews, boiled fish, bread and butter puddings and large jam tarts on Sundays. Bernard ate out as much as possible. Charlotte and Bernard had promised they would not quarrel, so he could not mention the cooking. Sometimes they sat quite tongue-tied; the compulsion to disagree was so strong they dared not exercise their tongues.

12

LOOKING out of my bedroom window, I saw that yellow leaves were falling from the chestnut trees like large yellow gloves. It was a late September Sunday and neatly-dressed members of the Salvation Army, carrying music cases and shimmering brass and silver instruments, hurried across the Green to their nearby citadel. There was a faint smell of chicken casserole floating up the stairs, which reminded me that Brit and Stephen were coming to lunch, Brit to say goodbye. "But we have good news for you too," she had said as she snatched the receiver from Stephen before he rang off. I had heard them laughing together and wondered if they were engaged to be married; they sounded so happy in spite of Brit's departure.

As I prepared the meal heavy rain began to fall and when they arrived they kissed me with wet faces. They sniffed around my steaming pots and pans as if they were starving, Brit even lifting the saucepan lids. It was then I noticed the ring on her left hand, a sapphire and two diamonds in a rather old-fashioned setting. I'd worn that ring myself for nearly a month so knew it well. Before that it had belonged to Stephen's mother. Brit held her hand close to my eyes as children do when they want to show you something. "Yes, we've been engaged for three days now," she said gaily. "That's our good news. How do you like my ring? It was Stephen's mother's and it means a lot to him."

I could hear a faint disappointment in her voice and guessed she would have preferred a new one that they had chosen together. I admired it and said, "I know that ring does mean a lot to him and he always planned to give it to the girl he intended to marry. He may have shown it to other girls, but he never let them try it on. I'm sure you are the first girl he has truly wanted to marry, and I don't blame him," and I gave her a friendly hug.

Stephen was sitting at the dining-table building a little wooden farm with Tommy but I could see he was intently listening and was pleased with my silly white lies. Fortunately my eyes hadn't flicked as they sometimes do when I'm not telling the truth—they were only small lies though. Later, when Brit and Tommy were upstairs playing a game that entailed a lot of laughing, I told Stephen he should have bought Brit a new engagement ring. Had he even asked her if she cared for sapphires? Perhaps she loved rubies, as I did, or flashing emeralds: but in any case she should have helped choose it.

At first Stephen was angry and said I was jealous and a "carper." Then he became miserable and said he wasn't too happy about the ring either, it didn't seem suitable for Brit somehow. But with all the expense of joining her in New York for Christmas and getting married, he dared not spend much on a ring.

"She's been showing it to all the cast and I noticed they didn't sound too enthusiastic—or perhaps it was just my guilty conscience. Oh God, what do you advise me to do? Buy her another?"

I thought for a moment and decided that two engagement rings would be absurd, so suggested a brooch or bracelet, perhaps antiques which would be untaxed. "Try the Burlington Arcade or somewhere similar, but go together; you'll enjoy it—except for the paying part, of course," I laughed.

"I suppose I am rather a mean bastard," Stephen said thoughtfully, "but I don't want to be mean with Brit. I love her far too much."

Brit left the following Wednesday and I closed the shop and went with Stephen to Heathrow to see her off. When we met her at the airport she was standing with a group of dancers, lovely girls but not so beautiful as Brit who was really outstanding. I made as if to leave her alone with Stephen, but they asked me to stay. They had already said their goodbyes and, as she lifted her slender hand to adjust her hair, I saw she was wearing a bracelet, a pretty thing decorated with garnets, and I smiled at Stephen approvingly.

Eventually Brit rejoined her dancing friends and disappeared into the departure lounge and Stephen made a rush to the nearest bar and drank a neat whisky. He stood there with his eyes closed for a few minutes, then grabbed my arm and said, "Let's go," and we hurried away into the real world. To me airports are a kind of limbo and the few times I've flown I've suffered from claustrophobia. I was glad to be back in my safe little shop with the sign on the door turned to "Open." I sold two brass elephants, an iron door-stop and a Bristol glass rolling-pin in quick succession in spite of the fact that Stephen was mooning around the shop with a fearful deprived expression on his face, giving deep sighs every now and again. He drifted away late in the afternoon and, although I was sorry for him, I was glad to see him go. Poor Stephen, it was almost as if he were acting his sorrow.

Tommy missed her weekends at the Forbeses'. She'd ask, "When are we going home? I want Gertrude, I want my swing, my garden, the dog. When's Bernard coming?" He sometimes paid us a short visit in the evening and Tommy would curl up on his knee and ask, "Are we going home, Bernard?"

I'd try to take her "home," even for a short time, at least once a week and she'd walk round the formal garden examining her favourite places: the little hut made of reeds the gardener had built for her, a grassy hill she liked to roll down, and of course, the swing. Then the dog had to be taken for a walk in the park, just a short walk because Tommy's legs were still rather small and the poor old dog was suffering from arthritic hips and soon tired. Sometimes Tommy would ask Gertrude to give her a bath but this she was unable to do. She appeared very tired to me.

She said it was the tiredness of waiting and of having her kind but bossy sister in the house all the time. "She'll be returning to the school next week. At least she'll be teaching there all day and only be here in the evenings. But then there is this Australian nurse, Marie she's called, and as soon as Charlotte goes, Marie comes. The doctor insists on it although the baby isn't due for at least a fortnight. Oh dear, I wouldn't admit it to anyone else but you, Bella, but I sometimes think I've been very inconsiderate having the baby born at home. Poor

Bernard, with all these women about the place. And poor me, for that matter! I could have gone into hospital as you did and be home within a week. It seemed more romantic to have one's first baby in one's own house and there's the blue and white plaque I've thought about so often. Sometimes I stand by that dear old stone lion looking up at the house and I can see it with "John Bernard Forbes born 1980" painted there. Perhaps it's just as well I can't see the second date, some time in 2,000, I suppose."

She had convinced us all that the baby would be a boy because she wanted one so much. Usually he was John Bernard, but occasionally he was Francis Bernard and for a short period Otto, after her father. I didn't care for Otto at all and thought of him as a weedy boy with ratty teeth, wearing wire-framed spectacles.

Mother telephoned to ask me to have lunch with her. Except that her voice was rather gruff, as it always was on the telephone, she was quite pleasant at first, asking after our health and that kind of thing, but by the time she mentioned lunch there was a distinct air of strain: "You won't come at the weekend, will you? Some time during the week would suit me, Wednesday for instance." I told her that would mean closing the shop and upsetting Tommy's routine at the nursery. "Routine? There's no need to upset her routine. Just take her to the nursery in the normal way and then come here by public transport. You've done it before."

I said, "You don't want me to bring Tommy, then?"

Mother's voice grew even gruffer. "To tell you the truth, I don't. My neighbours on the right, the Pickards, are fearfully nosy and a little black grandchild would spread down the road like wildfire. After all, I've been living here for twenty-seven years."

"And you can stay there for another twenty-seven for all I care, but I certainly won't be coming for lunch," and I crashed the receiver down, hoping the sound would burst my mother's eardrums. I was so angry, I could feel my scar throbbing and I imagined it had turned burning red. I looked at my reflection in a tarnished gilt mirror that never seemed to sell and saw that my scar was the same as usual, just silvery white and a little twisted.

Someone was rattling at the door, so I turned my eyes away from the mirror and saw it was Mary, standing there with her arms around a spelter bust. I was so pleased to see her lively face peering through her mop of dark hair. We examined the bust which was rather an attractive one. It was a reproduction of some classical figure, but neither of us could remember which it was—perhaps Minerva. Mary took off her soiled white raincoat, which reminded me of a dirty candle, and we sat together in the back room drinking tea. I told her my troubles, cried a little, sold a couple of Victorian prints all decorated with tinsel. Then we settled down to the shop's accounts in a leisurely way. In spite of the quietness of summer the shop had still made a reasonable profit.

13

IT WAS the end of September and I had been running the shop for over eight months, the happiest months of my life. My work suited me down to the ground, I had my dear little daughter to love and care for and a few good friends, and there were the Forbeses. They were almost more than friends. They had become a major influence in my life and had taught me so much it was as if I'd been reborn and I had lost much of my bitterness and lack of confidence. They had helped me to live with my scar. In a way I'd almost become fond of it because it was something I'd mastered. But I hadn't mastered my feelings towards my mother. Although at times things were a little easier between us, it didn't last. Bernard had met her and could see how difficult she was: but Gertrude was so gentle and kind she couldn't understand our antagonism towards each other, my mother's spiteful rejection and my anger at being rejected. Fortunately this period of my life was so full I had little time to brood over our relationship.

During September I did have one small worry—boys, particularly at weekends. They threw stones, large pieces of wood and even bricks at the horse-chestnut trees, trying to knock down the unripe conkers. One morning, quite a large stone came whizzing through one of the shop windows, shattering the glass. I didn't catch the boys and for two days was more or less trapped in the house until I could get someone to mend the window. The Green began to look like a battlefield, all strewn with broken branches, twigs and leaves. Then, when the chestnuts fell from the trees so glossy and perfect, the boys completely ignored them; but I noticed that many adults found them irresistible and left the Green with shopping bags and pockets bulging. I was one of the adults.

What with the broken window and the shop being rather busy I didn't see Gertrude for over a week, and when I did I noticed quite a change. She had grown even more dreamy and far away and had lost her interest in the garden; but had taken up painting in water colour and was illustrating a book of romantic German poems. She told me that she used to paint in her youth and now she had an urge to take it up again. She rinsed her brushes and said: "Bernard is so pleased about it and has showered me with paints. He thinks it's so safe, me sitting here and painting away at these lovely illustrations. But he doesn't know that I suck my brushes. I always have and believe it is quite deadly, at least, so they told me when I was a girl."

The illustrations really were rather lovely and painted with skill and I thought, if I could paint like that, I'd paint all the time and not just put it aside for years. Everything Gertrude did, she did with an effortless perfection. Even in late pregnancy her movements were graceful and her step as light as ever. Her look of tiredness had gone and been replaced by a kind of remote content.

We were sitting in the dining-room, with the long table all scattered with painting materials, when the young nurse came in with a tray of coffee things. I'd forgotten about the nurse and wondered who she was until Gertrude introduced us. Marie, she was called. At first I was puzzled by her accent and a certain air of assurance that I'd known before. Then I remembered the Australian girls I'd been friendly with in my bedsitter days; some of them had been nurses too. Gertrude had been expecting a bossy creature and was delighted with Marie although Bernard considered her too young for such an important role. "He would prefer a sergeant-major of a nurse with a row of medals on her chest," Gertrude laughed as she sipped her coffee. Then she replaced her cup in its saucer and, removing a turquoise ring from her little finger, she handed it to me. "It's for Marlinchen," she said almost apologetically. "My grandmother gave it to me when I was only a little older than she is and it is so silly for me to wear a child's ring. I've been meaning to give it to her for some time, well, ever since I knew I was to be a mother." She handed me the small gold ring, such a pretty thing, a circle of turquoises clustering round a small diamond—Edwardian I should imagine. I hardly liked to take it, but Gertrude insisted and she didn't like to be crossed, particularly now. So the ring was put in its dark velvet case and slipped into my handbag to be given to Marlinchen on her fifth birthday.

Before I left Marie joined us for a few minutes. She made a very good impression on me, particularly as I gathered that she was doing most of the cooking besides looking after Gertrude. I'd heard that nurses often expected to be waited on, but Marie was willing to do anything to help, including the shopping and taking the dog for a walk. She was engaged for a month, then returning to Australia—perhaps to be married, but she hadn't quite made up her mind about this because it was almost two years since she had seen her boyfriend and she wasn't sure how she felt about him. They frequently wrote, "But letters are not the same as being together," she said thoughtfully. "I've changed a lot since I've lived in England, grown up, I suppose, and he might have stayed the same. I'm not a virgin any more, for one thing." Slightly embarrassed she hurried from the room, the cups and saucers rattling on the tray.

I went home to collect Tommy from the nursery and found her dancing about impatiently because I was late and most of the children had already left. Now she was three she had rather outgrown the place. Although there were still children of her own age there, they were mostly placid types, quite happy to sit in small groups, sometimes hugging one of the nursery toys in their arms. They seldom snatched from each other but occasionally the boys had a mild fight. Quite often there were birthday parties.

Since her third birthday in August Tommy had started to develop rapidly, almost in jerks. She could count a little, recognized letters and could do simple puzzles without help. Suddenly her vocabulary increased and we were having almost intelligent conversations, and sometimes in the evening, when I was sitting looking a little dejected, she'd stroke my face and say, "Tired, mummy?" in a kind and grown-up way. She became more inventive too and persevered in making simple things work, turning keys in stiff locks and unscrewing jar lids, particularly honey-pot lids, climbing onto chairs so that she could reach things I didn't want her to touch, opening the fridge and taking what she fancied. Once I found her grating away at poor Teddy's fur with a cheese-grater and this really saddened me because it was the kind of thing my mother might have done as a child. I still remembered the horror of her turning my much-loved doll into a Frankenstein monster of a creature with a dark burnt arm and a terrible box-like body. Had she grated away at her teddy's soft fur when she was a child?

14

GERTRUDE'S baby was overdue and there was talk of an induce-
ment, but she refused to have one because she considered it unnatural and Bernard was inclined to agree with her. They reassured each
other by saying: "It's only five days, six days, seven days late." Then,
in the early hours of the morning on October the ninth, Gertrude
telephoned me to say that she was in labour and felt marvellous and,
although it was the middle of the night, she was walking about and
playing her favourite records, Mozart and Vivaldi, "His concerto in
D major for two trumpets is very helpful. Can you hear it?" she asked
excitedly. She promised to phone me again when the baby was safely
born. "About twelve o'clock in the morning after I've had a little sleep.
Labour pains are not so bad as I expected, but very deep and primitive, not like any other pain. Perhaps some women become addicted
to them and that's why they have so many children. Goodbye, dear
Bella. The doctor has just arrived, but I'll be in touch very soon." Her
voice sounded strong and full above the music and when I returned
to bed it was as if I could still hear the beautiful confident voice ringing in my head above the sound of Vivaldi's trumpets. That was the
last time I heard Gertrude's voice because she died early in the morning just as it was getting light. She and Bernard and their child had
less than twenty minutes together as a family.

Not knowing what had happened I waited all day for Gertrude
to telephone and by the time it was evening I was convinced that the
baby was born dead. Several times I held the receiver in my hand but
was unable to bring myself to dial the Forbeses' number. I couldn't
face any bad news that was waiting for me. Perhaps the longed-for

baby was deformed or very sickly or the labour pains were false ones. It never crossed my mind that Gertrude might have died.

The following morning when I went to open the shop Bernard was standing by his car. As he crossed the road he hardly noticed the on-coming traffic and horns were honking at him and the lollipop man was jumping up and down with frustration but he didn't notice: his eyes were like black holes and his face dark and unshaven. He told me not to open the shop, but to return with him to Richmond, so I shut the door behind me and went with him just as I was. We sat silent in the car for a few heavy minutes, then he said: "I suppose you know that Gertrude is dead. She died suddenly yesterday morning of a haemorrhage amongst other things. She was proudly holding the child and the happiness on her face . . . It was as if she'd died of happiness." He said no more and we drove away. It was so fearful there was nothing to say, we were like two sleep-drivers.

When we reached the house Bernard immediately took me upstairs and, as we stood outside the bedroom door, he said, "You would like to see her, wouldn't you? There's nothing to be afraid of, she looks beautiful, just as she always was." We went in and he put a hand on my shoulder, as if for support, and we gazed at Gertrude, lying like a statue and looking very much as she had the first time I saw her in the snowy courtyard. There was no baby in her arms, so perhaps it was still alive. "The baby," I asked. "What has happened to the baby?"

"Oh, the baby," he said vaguely. "I suppose it's with Marie."

As we spoke there came the bleating cry of a new-born child from the next room, the nursery that Gertrude had prepared months ago. Bernard still stood looking down at his wife, so I took his cold hand and walked towards the door, looking back once for a last glance at Gertrude's pale profile. Then we went into the other room.

The nurse, Marie, was feeding the child from a small bottle and I could see by her inflamed eyes that she had been crying. She told me that the baby was a boy and weighed nearly nine pounds and he certainly was a fine child, with an exceptionally white skin and rose-red cheeks, looking much older than his two days. When he had finished his bottle she put him in my arms. I felt a strange revulsion to him. It was partly because he was the cause of Gertrude's death, but it wasn't only that, it was his colouring. The contrast of the snow-white skin and the rose-red cheeks was so unusual in a new-born baby. I tried to pass him on to Bernard, but he backed away saying, "No, no, not yet." He stroked the baby's soft bright hair for a moment and then quickly left the room.

He was waiting on the landing for me and jerked out, "His name is John, you know."

I corrected him: "John Bernard, isn't it?"

He agreed: "Yes, John Bernard, poor little fellow. At the moment I can't really feel for him. He doesn't seem real to me somehow and I expect him to vanish. I can't bear to hear him cry. Charlotte will drive you home. It's all arranged," and he stumbled away from me, his unshaven face all wet with tears. I'd never been close to death before and it was far worse than I'd imagined, particularly sudden death.

Gertrude was cremated, as she would have wished to be, although Charlotte and Bernard would have preferred a grave where they could plant her favourite flowers. I went to the funeral but slipped away before it ended because I didn't want to be there when she was burnt and reduced to tiny ashes and smoke came out of a narrow chimney, as I'd heard. I went home and opened the shop as if nothing had happened and because I didn't care one way or another I sold a Victorian sofa that had been filling the shop for months. In the evening Mary came to see me and we went to the nearest pub together, leaving Tommy alone in the house, a thing I'd never done before. I'd have got drunk if it would have helped, but after two Guinnesses I felt worse than I did before. Being so black, Guinness is a suitable drink for funerals, but I couldn't imagine Bernard serving it.

It was over three weeks before I saw Bernard again and I was beginning to think he had dropped me. After all, I was really Gertrude's friend and he had only been interested in improving my mind and as someone to keep Gertrude amused. Then, one Saturday evening as I was re-arranging the shop window, Tommy suddenly cried, "Bernard's coming." She always seemed to know when he was coming before he appeared. We were standing together, looking hopefully through the window, when his car drew up beside the Green and, seeing our eager faces, he smiled at us in a normal way. I'd been imagining him as I'd last seen him, broken and unshaven, his upper lip drawing back from his teeth every now and then.

We went into the back room together and he sat in his usual chair which I'd never liked to sell because we called it Bernard's chair and Tommy curled up on his knee like a contented kitten and we sat there in the dusk, drinking rather inferior sherry and talking in low tones. He told me that Charlotte had given up her teaching for the time being so that she could look after the baby and run the house after Marie left. It was a noble thing to do because she enjoyed her work and independence and was giving it up for the restricted life of a mother-housekeeper. "Thank God we still have old Mrs. Hicks coming in to do the cleaning, but for how long, we don't know. She adored Gertrude and it isn't so easy for her to work for Charlotte; the sisters have such different temperaments, or rather, had. Poor Charlotte, she tries so hard not to quarrel with me. I almost miss our battles."

He wasn't with us for long but it was arranged that Tommy and I would stay in Richmond the following weekend. "You'll have to face it sometime, my dear. I know the house is just a shell of a place without her, but you want to see Johnny, don't you? We call him Johnny now, but I don't know if Gertrude would have approved. Better than Otto, I suppose, but anything she liked to call him would seem perfect to me."

I had seen little of Stephen since Brit returned to the States. He'd telephoned a few times and called once when I was out and once when I was at home; but he had been in a restless mood and didn't stay long. Somehow, not through me, he heard about Gertrude's death and came to see me immediately. He'd never met her but knew how much the friendship meant to me and, although he teased me about the "pompous Bernard," he never joked about Gertrude. I think they would have got on very well because people were always at their best with her and Stephen at his best could be very charming. He was at his best that evening and did all he could to comfort me. Brit wasn't mentioned once the entire evening and he bought me flowers and Chinese food, which we nibbled sitting on the floor in front of the gas fire. That night we went to bed together, more as friends than lovers. It was a thing that occasionally happened between us at times of stress, a way of comforting each other that was in no way a commitment.

Bernard came to fetch us the following Saturday as we had arranged and there was Tommy jumping around us and talking about Gertrude and the swim in the bath she was looking forward to, the swing and the toys waiting in her bedroom, the dog and the carved bear guarding the house in the courtyard. She hadn't been to the Forbeses' house for weeks and had missed it sorely, poor child, but I was so on edge I could have hit her. Instead I covered my scar with my hand, a thing I hadn't done for months. Bernard gently removed my hand and slipped it into my pocket, saying in the kindest way: "Relax, you silly girl. It won't be as terrible as you imagine. There's Johnny, for one thing, and we have been so looking forward to you coming."

I smiled at the thought of Charlotte looking forward to my visit. Usually she hardly noticed me and I couldn't remember a single conversation between us, just "Hallo," "Goodbye," "It's very warm," "It's very cold," and surprisingly "What a dear little girl you have. Is she adopted?" Yet, there she was, standing on the doorstep with a welcoming smile on her fine face and a kiss on both cheeks for me and a hug for Tommy-Marline, who ran into the house looking for Gertrude although I'd already explained to her that she was away. "Has she gone to the shops?" she asked and all I could think of saying was that she had gone very far away where there were no shops and she had taken Petra the dog with her. Petra had died in her sleep a few days after Gertrude. Mrs. Hicks had found her lying under the kitchen table, but as she often lay there, hadn't realized she was dead until there was no response to a bowl of her favourite food. Then, being a quiet woman who disliked scenes, she had knocked on Bernard's door and said, "Please, sir, the dog appears to have died. It's making no movement."

Marie was putting Johnny to bed when we all trouped in to see him. There he was, sitting on her knee and looking at us with Gertrude's beautiful eyes. He was very large and handsome and exactly the sort of baby she had wished for, but, as Marie put him in my arms, again I had the slight revulsion to him although his very white skin and rose-red cheeks appeared more natural now. His Aunt Charlotte had very much the same colouring. Bernard obviously doted on the child and his eyes never left him, but he did not hold him in his arms—perhaps he was too shy in the presence of three eager women and a transfixed little girl. From the moment Marline saw the beautiful child she adored him as if he had been her own baby brother, which indeed she thought he was, and she never showed the slightest trace of jealousy.

On the surface we got through the weekend without too much suffering; but there were some painful moments. Once, when Bernard and I were walking together in the garden, we came across Gertrude's half-tame magpies chattering on a low bough of the juniper tree and they looked at us with clever eyes as if they knew that she was dead. We were both aware of something almost sinister and I, who was often afraid to touch people, clutched Bernard's arm and buried my face in his shoulder so that I couldn't see their knowing eyes. We were both shaking.

On Sunday evening we couldn't bring ourselves to play Gertrude's records, or any records for that matter, so we settled for Scrabble. I wondered where the Scrabble had come from, Charlotte perhaps. The Forbeses didn't play games, with the exception of chess. I was quite enjoying the game when Bernard, who was winning, suddenly jumped up, scattering the letters, muttered something about "Damn fool game" and left the room.

On Monday, when he was driving us back to Twickenham, he stopped the car near Marble Hill and apologized for the Scrabble incident. "It's Charlotte trying to be a ray of sunshine that gets me down, although I know she means it for the best. The other day she suggested brightly that I went for a nice walk in the park with the dog; she'd forgotten that she had been dead for three weeks or more—poor creature, nothing to live for, like me. I sometimes feel that I'm harnessed to remorse, misery and loneliness for the rest of my life. I can't see how it can ever get better. There's Johnny, of course, but it will be years until I can really talk to him. I watch him, though, and he's changing all the time. He has Gertrude's eyes, have you noticed? And Marie says he's very advanced for his age. My poor Gertrude, how she would have loved him."

Tommy was becoming restless in her little seat in the back of the car so we drove on and, just as we were half way down Heath Road and were held up in the traffic, I suddenly remembered a beautiful August day when Gertrude and I were in the flowery thicket and she had made me promise to look after her baby if anything happened to her. I'd forgotten all about it; but now, in this ugly, traffic-filled road, it came back to me with great clarity and it was as if we were still in the Burning Bush Restaurant, under the juniper tree with the magpies moving about in the branches above, and I was making this serious promise.

I turned to Bernard, who was frowning at the almost stationary traffic, and cried, "Oh, Bernard, I've just remembered I promised Gertrude I'd look after her child if anything happened to her. How could I have forgotten?"

Bernard's frowning face relaxed as he turned towards me: "Of course I know you will do anything humanly possible for Gertrude's child, whether you have made promises or not. You are absolutely trustworthy, Bella, dear."

Then the traffic cleared and we drove on. Now I felt doubly committed to little John Bernard.

15

I HADN'T seen Miss Murray for several months. Then she turned up at the shop like a fairy godmother with her usual large basket filled with damaged china. She had heard about Gertrude's death and thought going through the china would cheer me up. She knew the Forbeses fairly well and called Gertrude a headstrong woman because she had insisted on having her baby at home. "She would have been pushing her baby through the streets like any other woman if she had gone into hospital. Having a baby at home was so foolhardy at her age, don't you agree?" Then, relenting, "I might have done the same, though."

"It's a very fine child," I said listlessly as I picked over her rejects. Then, with more interest, "I like these Italian cups with the cupids. They seem perfect to me."

She examined them for a moment. "Well, they're on the heavy side, don't you think? And there are only three of them. No one wants three cups, it's six or perhaps four or even two. I know, sell them as a pair and keep the odd one yourself."

I smiled and said I'd keep one for my early morning cup of tea, and I drank from it for many mornings.

It is strange how that Italian cup comforted me and helped me back on the right track again. I've noticed that after a crisis in one's life or a bad illness quite a small thing can be the turning point towards recovery. I can remember having pneumonia as a child. It must have been when my father was still with us because he seemed to be sitting there night and day and trying to get me to eat a kind of meat jelly called Brand's Essence; but I turned my face away and demanded celery. I had a craving for it and the doctor eventually allowed me to chew—but not swallow—beautiful, crisp celery, and from that moment I recovered rapidly. The Italian cup acted in the same way and I began to take an interest in the shop again. I bought a new winter overcoat and made an appointment with an expensive hairdresser to have my dark hair re-styled. I even went to a Sunday morning party given by one of Stephen's friends and I quite enjoyed it.

The thing I did not enjoy was my bi-weekly visit to the Forbeses' house. Tommy and I went there every other weekend and Tommy was happy enough playing with the baby in the nursery and "helping" Marie push the pram and was becoming quite attached to Charlotte. Charlotte was trying to take Gertrude's place, but she lacked Gertrude's charm. She was very friendly towards me and even asked my advice about babies and household things and occasionally about Bernard. She would say, "He's so fond of you, he'd do anything for you. He thinks of you almost like a daughter. What was it I said that upset him so at lunch? Why did he leave most of his prunes, doesn't he like them? And the Vivaldi record. Why tear it from the machine and stamp on it? Such beautiful music and one of Gertrude's favourites." She never spoke to me about anything intellectual although she quite rightly prided herself on her good brain. She seemed to think mine was entirely domestic and if I came out with a remark about surrealist paintings, for instance, she would say, "Well, well, who's talking." I'm sure she didn't mean to be unkind but she didn't understand people and their feelings.

Bernard suffered more than I did because he had her every day and couldn't see the end of it. "She's so insensitive, that's the trouble, and she looks very like Gertrude at times, which makes it worse. Oh God, what am I saying? She has given up the work she loves, she's doing everything she can to help and all I do is criticize her. I must start taking her to concerts again, she enjoys them and we get on much better when there is something serious to talk about." He drew me to him and said, "And as for you, my little one, we must continue your education. There's a new play I'd particularly like you to see and I still haven't taken you to a concert. Perhaps we should start with Schubert."

After Bernard started taking us out again life was not so gloomy and we all got on together much better. Charlotte was very generous about looking after Marline, when Bernard took me out on my mind-improving evenings, and in return I sometimes helped her with the cooking, particularly when Bernard's business associates came to dinner.

Marie had stayed on for nearly two extra months and was fretting to return to Australia so another nurse had to be found. Bernard was in favour of an old-fashioned nanny but Charlotte thought she would need to be waited on and it would mean meals on trays and that kind of thing so they eventually chose quite a young girl called Nell who turned out to be cheerful and kind but Bernard objected to her clothes. She was suitably dressed for the interview but must have hired or borrowed the neat, dark clothes because after the first day they never appeared again. She constantly wore crumpled jeans and T-shirts, usually with messages printed across the chest, and the thing that really upset Bernard was that every time she bent down, and one is always bending down when looking after young children, a large bare gap appeared between her shirt and jeans. Quite a nice piece of back but Bernard and Charlotte both objected to it.

Suddenly Christmas loomed, my first Christmas in the shop on the Green. Customers began to ask for small things like glass paper-weights and Staffordshire china and plates that could be hung on the wall. Large dishes suitable for turkeys were much in demand too. I spent my free Mondays searching for small treasures and to my great joy found a family of Edwardian dolls wearing their original clothes; otherwise it was mostly pretty little jugs, muffin dishes and silver jewellery, all very saleable at that time.

With Christmas coming I began to have guilty feelings towards my mother. Should I send her a card or present or even go and see her? I knew Gertrude would urge me to if she were still alive, but I kept putting it off. Then the problem was solved because mother telephoned one evening and in her abrupt way announced that she was calling the following afternoon. "Of course I shall expect to see my *Brazilian* grandchild," she said and banged the receiver down without mentioning Mr. Crimony. As she had such a low opinion of London transport it was unlikely she would come without her tame chauffeur. Although it was late in the evening I hurried to the kitchen and made a six-egg sponge cake and it rose beautifully and stayed that way. Some of my cakes came out of the oven looking perfect, but as soon as I turned my back on them they sank in the middle.

I fetched Tommy home early from the nursery. We ran back across the Green together just in time to see a red Rover drawing up outside the shop. Out of it stepped my Mother, but there was no sign of Mr. Crimony. We watched her collect some parcels from the boot of the car and make sure the car was safely locked before she crossed the road. She looked back at it with such a look of pride on her usually severe face that it even lingered a little when she saw us.

Altogether the visit passed off better than I had expected. There was the car to talk about, the driving lessons and the test, which she passed with flying colours—"and to think I could have been driving all these years. Mr. Crimony says I'm a born driver, except when I lose my temper with other drivers, of course."

Tommy said, "Where is he, the man called Mr. Chimney?"

Mother laughed. "Mr. Crimony, you mean. Well, he couldn't come today but has sent you a present." Then, turning to me, "He's having his feet done. Poor man, he suffers with them a lot. In the summer his feet feel the heat and he has to wear charcoal in his socks, and in the winter it's arthritis and ingrowing toenails. Now, what about these presents?"

I was touched by the presents, all wrapped in Christmas paper. A handknitted pullover for Tommy, and the right size too, so mother must have thought about her as she knitted away in Kilburn. Very expensive-looking suède gloves for me and the promised violin for Tommy, also a large golden-haired doll, both from Mr. Crimony. Mother said he had chosen the doll himself. It had its own hairdressing kit and was about as vulgar as a doll could possibly be, but fortunately Tommy thought it beautiful. Just before leaving, mother thrust another present into Tommy's eager hands. When unwrapped it turned out to be a golliwog.

A few days before Christmas Stephen left for the States to marry Brit. Somehow I'd never really expected this to happen, particularly as Stephen hardly mentioned her for weeks, perhaps just to save my feelings. It seemed so final, his going so far away. I went with him to Heathrow to see him off and was almost glad when he announced that he had no English money with him and would need me to pay for his excess baggage. It was only nine pounds; but he appeared to have plenty of English notes when he paid for our taxi a few minutes before. I'd almost forgotten his little meannesses. Now I remembered how mad they used to make me when we lived together.

As we parted I said, "Goodbye, old Meanie." Then we kissed each other and I said, "Goodbye, dearest old Meanie," and he said, "Goodbye, dearest little Scarface," and he hurried away towards the departure lounge. We never saw each other again. There were letters, but as Marie said, letters aren't the same.

16

GERTRUDE'S ashes rather weighed on my mind, lightly, but they weighed. Had Bernard already sprinkled them in the thicket or were they still in their silver box, waiting for a suitable occasion, Christmas perhaps? Would it be a solitary scattering or a gathering of family and friends? Eventually I asked Charlotte, only to find that she was as puzzled as I was. "The only thing I know is that they are still in their silver box in Bernard's study. Actually, I polish it sometimes and would know if it were empty, but they have never been mentioned between us. It could be that he can't bear to part with them." She drew her hair back from her strong, smooth forehead and added, "All I do know is that it would cause a hell of a rumpus if I mentioned them, don't you agree?" I agreed and we didn't speak of them again, even to each other.

Bernard seemed to take it for granted that we were to spend Christmas at Richmond, although it wouldn't be a very happy occasion for adults. I'd hoped that Tommy and I would have a quiet one of our own, with no complications; but it turned out that we had to spend three days of sad celebrations. Even Nell, who had never known Gertrude, was downcast. We exchanged silly presents wrapped in gaudy paper, and Charlotte and I cooked a great meal; but we could just as well have served mutton chops, no one was hungry. At least we didn't have crackers. Marline was disappointed about this but otherwise was happy opening and playing with her presents, and there was Johnny lying in his carry-cot before the fire.

Already he was lifting his head and trying to look round the room, and he had the sweetest smile. Bernard loved to watch him and sometimes held out a finger to be clasped in the soft baby hand; but he seldom held him in his arms. On the other hand, I, who loved the child with reservations, often sat with him on my lap or held him against my shoulder with his little face against mine. He was a very comforting baby and seldom cried. Nell looked after him well, in spite of her bare back, which did not appear quite so often now the cold weather had set in.

It was a relief when the twelve days of Christmas were over and I didn't have to keep closing the shop for unwanted holidays. The auction sales picked up again and at one I bid for a table that looked like a mahogany sofa table. It was heavily disguised with dirty cream paint and, as no one else saw through the disguise, I bought it for very little. When I got the table home and was able to examine it at leisure I saw that I was right. Wearing rubber gloves, Mary and I tried to remove the offending paint, but it was beyond us and we had to take it to a nearby workshop and have it removed professionally. This proved expensive, but even then we made a large profit, which was good for my ego as well as my bank account. I felt how fortunate I was to be able to earn a living doing something I so enjoyed and I really loved the little shop. Perhaps it was a bit of a tie sometimes, but I could always close it for a few hours. It wasn't like an ordinary job and Mary absolutely trusted me and never interfered.

Really, the only problem of a practical nature I had at this time was Tommy's education. She was definitely too old for the nursery and thoroughly bored with it, and although there were three state schools within walking distance, they were for older children. Eventually I found a privately-run playschool which suited her very well. She enjoyed the simple lessons and the company of slightly older children, so it was well worth paying the extra money. But we missed running across the Green and feeding the birds every morning. Instead we had a long wait for a bus to take us quite a short journey. When Bernard heard about this he bought me a gleaming new bicycle with a small seat for Tommy fixed on the carrier, so another problem was solved.

Although I missed Gertrude terribly and Stephen in a lesser way, this was a rewarding and peaceful time of my life. Tommy was well settled, I had a slightly better relationship with my mother, the shop was thriving, I enjoyed my outings with Bernard and my visits to Richmond were no longer to be dreaded. Bernard and Charlotte seemed to be getting on better together and the clouds of sorrow had slightly lifted from the house. Charlotte could listen to records without fear of them being ripped from the machine and stamped on. But Bernard was working hard and spent a lot of the weekends shut in his study or with Peter, his assistant, who had a studio and a workshop in the house although one seldom came across him. During the week Bernard stayed late at his gallery in Dover Street and Charlotte complained: "It is as if he doesn't want to come home any more now Gertrude has gone. I'm sure he would sell the house and live in a flat if it weren't for Johnny. Sometimes he says he hates it because Gertrude is here no more, then at other times he says the house is sacred because she once lived here. Her clothes are all hanging in the cupboards, you know, and Mrs. Hicks got into fearful trouble because she threw away a half-empty pot of cold cream that was collecting dust on the dressing-table. It's not like him to be so morbid."

Sometimes on Mondays, when I closed the shop, Bernard would take me to art exhibitions and afterwards we would lunch together and discuss the paintings we had seen. Often we ate in expensive restaurants but at other times in places that were almost workmen's cafés, smelling of frizzling chip potatoes—it depended where the exhibitions were held and our mood. But wherever we went, I loved it. Occasionally Bernard would take me to a sale room and ask me to bid for some painting in my amateur way, usually a painting that he didn't want other dealers to know he was interested in. This made me feel like the mouse in the fable, who helped the lion. Only once did I bid for the wrong painting. I thought Bernard told me not to bid more than a hundred pounds for a dim-looking seascape and to my surprise I got it for only three. It was quite a different seascape that he wanted; but at least the gilt frame was worth far more than three pounds, so I hadn't made such a fearful mistake and it gave us something to laugh about.

Just when things seemed to be going rather well at the Richmond house there was trouble with Nell. It was something worse than a few inches of bare back this time. One weekend, when I was staying at the house, Bernard, Charlotte and I returned home earlier than we had expected after a particularly dull dinner party given by some kindly people who thought we needed "cheering up." As soon as we entered the house we could hear Johnny's piteous cry and it sounded as if it had been going on for some time. We ran upstairs and found him wailing in his cot, his cheeks all wet and his nappy in a bad state. There was a scrabbling sound from the next room where Nell slept, then stifled voices. Charlotte burst open the communicating door without even knocking and switched on the hard electric light to reveal a naked young man struggling into a T-shirt with "I'll tell the world" stamped across it and a startled Nell trying to wrap herself up in a sheet.

She pushed past Charlotte muttering with a yawn, "Sorry about that. I must have dropped off," then bending over the baby. "Oh my God. What a mess you're in!"

Bernard made to leave the room and bumped straight into the young man kneeling on the landing, trying to put on his socks and shoes. Bernard snarled, "Get out of my house or I'll kick you down the stairs. Charlotte, telephone the police."

The word "police" seemed to terrify the young man because he shot down the stairs and out of the house leaving the front door open, swinging in the winter wind. Bernard threw the shoes and smelly looking socks after him and there they remained on the pavement until the road-sweeper swept them away in the morning. Afterwards we learnt that he was a South American waiter whose permit had expired nearly two years previously and he particularly wanted to keep clear of the police.

On Monday morning, as Bernard drove us home, he said in a casual way, "I suppose you wouldn't give up the shop and look after Johnny instead? Of course, I'd make it worth your while."

Feeling a selfish monster, I refused his offer in spite of all the kindness and friendship I'd received. I couldn't give up my present life which suited me so well. Bernard took my refusal very calmly and said it was only an idea that had suddenly come into his mind—he hadn't even mentioned it to Charlotte. But I still felt guilty.

A middle-aged nanny was engaged to look after Johnny. She was absolutely reliable and a kindly woman, they said. But Johnny didn't love her as he had loved Nell. He'd thrived in her rather slapdash care and had looked on her as a mother, and now there was this sudden change. Charlotte did her best, but she wasn't really at home with babies, it was older children she was interested in. Johnny cried a lot the first two weeks in nanny's care, then he settled down and became a rather reserved baby who seldom smiled, except when my daughter was around every other weekend. Even then they didn't see as much of each other as they used to and it appeared to me that nanny kept the children apart. Marline wasn't included in the stately walks, with nanny deliberately pushing the large perambulator she insisted on using in spite of Richmond's steep hill and often crowded pavements. Sometimes I saw her charging through the town and it looked as if she were about to mow down any pedestrian that got in her way.

It took me some time to realize that nanny didn't approve of my poor little Tommy-Marline and that she didn't want to be seen in the streets with her and preferred not to have her in the nursery, although it was rather difficult to keep her out of it. If I were there she'd mutter remarks like, "I was really engaged to look after one child, not two," or, "It's better for Marline to leave baby alone; she only excites him." Sometimes Nell and I had bathed the children together surrounded by floating toys; but when I suggested this to nanny she was appalled. "Certainly not," she said. "It might end in a nasty accident." But what she really meant was that the darkness of my daughter's skin might contaminate the water.

I tried to conceal nanny's aversion to Marline from Bernard and Charlotte because it would only create bad feeling and could even cause nanny's dismissal and another change for Johnny. But it hurt me when Bernard said, "Why doesn't Marlinchen go for walks with Johnny any more? She seems to have lost interest in him and is hardly ever in the nursery these days."

I said, "I think she is a little shy of nanny because she has never met a real British nanny before. She is happy enough with Johnny when they are downstairs together." And so they were when nanny wasn't in the room. Even then I felt that I might have said too much and that Bernard was growing aware of nanny's antipathy.

Then one Sunday afternoon, when she was arranging Johnny in his great perambulator, Marline came running out of the house, struggling into her duffle coat: "Wait for me, nanny, let me come too."

Bernard and I were standing by the gate and heard Nanny say crossly: "Certainly not. One child is all I can manage on these hills and I don't want you chattering all the time."

Marline finished her struggle with the duffle coat. "But I won't chatter, I'll help. I'll push really hard."

Nanny said coldly, "I think you would be more of a hindrance than a help. Shut the gate after me, please." And she sailed through with this great pram before her, even ignoring Bernard.

Marline turned her quivering little face away and walked dejectedly towards the house, her red stockings twisted round her skinny legs adding to her piteous aspect. Bernard hurried after her and caught her up in his arms and said they were going for a walk in the park together—and I asked her if I was allowed to come too, which she thought very funny. So we went to the park together and froze in the early March wind. Neither of us had waited to put on coats; but it was worth being cold to see Marline happy again—even the twisted stockings looked rather jolly now.

A week or two later Charlotte was putting linen away in the great chest on the landing when she heard nanny ordering Marline out of the nursery. The door was open and Charlotte said she had one large hand on Marline's shoulder and was saying in a threatening way: "How many times have I told you I don't want you in here interfering with baby? I won't have him contaminated. Go down to the kitchen, that's the best place for you. But remember, I don't want to see you in here again." She gave her a final push through the door, then slammed it. Charlotte took Marline by the hand and ran down the stairs with her to tell Bernard what had happened and ask his advice. I was in the town at the time doing some weekend shopping and returned to find nanny had been dismissed and was sulking in her bedroom, Charlotte, with Johnny clasped in her arms, was crying and there was Bernard looking fearfully gloomy, with a glass of brandy in his hand, Bernard who drank little and never in the afternoon. Even the log fire had gone out and the room smelt of bitter smoke. But Marline was happily sitting on a pile of cushions munching chocolate biscuits, quite oblivious of the general air of despair around her.

17

By the time Johnny Forbes was seven months old he had had four different nurses. The last and best was a Spanish girl called Catalina, who had settled into the household far better than we had expected although her English was poor and Charlotte and Bernard did not know a word of Spanish. The main thing in her favour was that both the children loved her from the day she arrived with her scarlet imitation leather suitcases. She was a good-looking girl, with beautiful dark eyes glowing in her slightly heavy face. Her hands were soft and dimpled, very feminine. In some ways she resembled me in appearance. She had the same thick, dark hair that fell into good shapes and the fine white skin—but, of course, without my scar. Our figures were similar too, a little on the heavy side. My legs were longer than hers, but she made up for this by usually wearing very high-heeled shoes on her small, pretty feet. The thing that appealed to us all, including Johnny, was her warmth and cheerfulness: she was like a dear little fire warming our rather sad hearts.

Now Johnny was all smiles and already trying to crawl. He had been like a little zombie under nanny's care, and a clockwork zombie at that. Now time meant little in his life. If he awoke early in the morning, Catalina took him into her own bed and played with him. He had no fixed time for rests during the day, he just fell asleep when he felt tired, and in the evenings his bedtime varied from around seven to ten o'clock. Charlotte did insist on him having his meals at regular times that fitted in with ours and Catalina soon saw the wisdom of this. She liked to dress the children up before taking them out and sometimes they were drenched with "colonia," and Marline had her hair drawn up into a little topknot decorated with beads, looking odd but very sweet.

Monday was Catalina's day off and Charlotte said she spent hours over her toilet before she left the house. She would meet her Spanish friends in London and they would go from shop to shop until they closed. Then they'd go in a group to some friend's bedsitting-room and have a picnic meal and play records, the group growing larger and larger. Sometimes she gave her friends a miss and I took her to places of interest like the London Museum, Hampton Court or Buckingham Palace and the Houses of Parliament. Unfortunately she wasn't interested in art galleries or most museums and we often ended up looking in shop windows or spending an hour or more in Harrods, her favourite shop. At least twice a week Charlotte gave her an English lesson which they both enjoyed, particularly Charlotte, who loved to teach. Bernard, not to be outdone, tried to interest her in paintings and she said they were all "*Muy bonito*" and gave a pretty smile. Then he tried classical records, without much success. She would listen with her head a little on one side and a simulated expression of interest on her charming face, but all too soon she'd say she could hear Johnny crying and bolt from the room. Bernard, who had read some Spanish literature in translation, tried to discuss books with her; but the only book she was interested in was *Don Quixote*, which she insisted was true. "I've seen the window Dulcinea looked out of, Mr. Bernard, I've visited La Mancha with my cousins. Of course it's true." And she laughed at Bernard's ignorance. Quite soon he left her education to Charlotte, which pleased me because I was becoming a little jealous. I looked on myself as Bernard's special pupil and did not want to share my teacher.

It gradually happened that Marline and I spent most weekends in Richmond. They seemed to need my help there and we were made to feel very welcome. Marline was happier there than in the shop and she had come rather to despise the small park where we used to feed the ducks on sunny Sundays. When the weather was bad we spent most of the time shut up in the room behind the shop where I cooked and we ate and lived and occasionally looked at black and white television. But we preferred to climb the twisting staircase and from the upstairs windows we would look down on the traffic and people splashing round the Green exercising their dogs, the well fed pigeons and the seagulls skimming over the grass as if they were on wheels. On special days we'd see a squirrel darting about in the tree in front of the house. I really loved our little house, but it did feel rather cramped after Bernard's stately home.

On the other hand, he had become quite fond of our simple cottage and, I hoped, fond of us too. He visited us quite frequently in the evenings before he went home. He seldom stayed more than an hour and, if my daughter was already in bed, he'd sit in his special chair and I'd sit very close in some chair that was perhaps already sold and waiting to be collected. We'd sit there sometimes hardly speaking, and occasionally he would absent-mindedly stroke my hair as if I were a cat. Other times he would talk about his business and paintings he hoped to buy or sell and associates I knew nothing about. He could almost have been talking in a foreign language, I understood so little, and I had the feeling that he was really talking to Gertrude. He would say things like, "You remember that painting we half hoped was a Gustave Moreau; well, it definitely isn't. I must tell you what old Harrison said about it, it'd amuse you, darling. You know how outspoken he is." And he would ask my advice about having the house redecorated or renewing the lease of his gallery. He didn't seem to notice that I remained silent except for an occasional "Yes" or "No." Indeed, he would have been very surprised if I'd given advice of any kind. Although I did not understand all that Bernard was saying it made me extraordinarily happy that he should confide in me. I really honoured him; there was no other word for it.

On a spring morning when Charlotte and I were drinking coffee in the drawing-room with the windows open to the sun and birdsong, Bernard came in with Johnny in his arms and handing him to Charlotte said he wanted us all in the garden. Then he dived back into his study—I thought for a camera to take our photographs, but it was the silver box filled with Gertrude's ashes he was holding when he returned. As if in a dream I collected Marline from the swing and we followed Charlotte carrying the baby and Bernard to the edge of the thicket where the cherry and apple trees were in blossom. Bernard gently scattered some of the ashes there and the rest on and around the juniper tree in Gertrude's special place, just as she had wished. And as the ashes fell around, both the magpies settled on the little tree and watched us silently for a few moments. The hen then returned to her nest, but the cock magpie stayed watching us with his bright, knowing eyes.

Bernard said, "I've been waiting for a day like this, the kind of day she loved so much. She'd have been pleased about the birds too." He spoke quietly, as if to himself, but not with great grief.

The scattering of the ashes was a symbol, the fulfilment of a promise; but it did not ease his sorrow, which was with him all the time. Charlotte was openly crying and, seeing that Marline was about to follow her example, I took her by the hand and quickly walked away before she started asking where Gertrude was, as she did from time to time. At first I used to tell her that she had gone to Germany to join her mother, but Bernard did not approve of this feeble lie and told her firmly that Gertrude had gone away for ever. It was a relief to me that the ashes had now been scattered where Gertrude had wanted them to be and that it had turned out to be such a simple ceremony, even with a kind of charm. I didn't know at the time that some of Gertrude's ashes had already been sprinkled in a German garden that used to belong to her parents. All I knew was how beautiful Bernard's hands had looked as he scattered, one holding the silver box and the other scattering.

18

CHARLOTTE began to wilt and say it was time she had a holiday. She longed to travel around Germany and Belgium and visit various members of her family she had not seen for several years and she confided to me that she wanted to be free of responsibility. It had all come on suddenly: one day she was a happy teacher in her early thirties with her own little flat and the next she was in charge of a large house with servants to manage and a baby to help look after. "I've never cared for domestic life. Of course I love little Johnny, he's adorable, and I'm fond of Bernard; but I'm so tired, mentally and physically. Have you noticed, I haven't even the heart to argue with Bernard these days? Well, we did have a little quarrel about Kitaj's paintings and Bernard insisted he came here as a GI during the war—most unlikely, I think. But that was over a week ago. I really must get away." And, looking at her, I could see she was right. The colour seemed to have drained away from her and she was almost as pale as Gertrude used to be, but without her classical beauty.

At last it was arranged that she would be away for three weeks in July and that I was to live in the house during her absence. Bernard would fetch Tommy and me from the shop every evening and bring us back in the mornings on his way to his gallery. Mrs. Hicks, in spite of an invalid husband, agreed to work for extra hours and Catalina to shop and help generally besides looking after Johnny. I was to be responsible for running the house and planning the meals and cooking the dinner in the evening. Fortunately I knew the kind of food Bernard liked and had often helped Gertrude prepare the meals.

Johnny was more of a problem. There would be whole days when

Catalina was out. I didn't mind giving a helping hand when she was in charge of him, but my heart did sink at the thought of being completely responsible. Often Catalina was still bouncing him on her knee until ten o'clock at night. Suppose he choked on a hair-clip—mine were always falling from my hair—or he could have one of the frightful crying fits he sometimes indulged in, and the nappies were quite different to the towelling ones Marline had had. Johnny wore huge fluffy things like blown-up sanitary towels. I certainly wasn't looking forward to taking Charlotte's place in the household and running the shop at the same time.

And of course, after Charlotte left the shop was neglected and on some days not opened at all. Mary Meadows helped when she could and Miss Murray provided a basket of charming but chipped Victorian china. Bernard also gave me a lot of picture frames that were not up to his standard and, although they didn't improve the appearance of the shop, they sold quite easily. Relying on a lift from Bernard as I had to do meant that I often arrived late and left early. Some days there wasn't time to arrange the window as I liked it and there was no time to search for new stock. Still, it was only for three weeks, and I had promised Gertrude I would look after her child.

I often reminded myself of this promise; it had a habit of slipping to the back of my mind. Poor little Johnny, I did love him in a way and it wasn't so difficult looking after him as I had expected, no swallowed hair-clips or anything like that. However, there was one fatal day when I was left in sole charge of him and he cried almost non-stop. It wasn't only that he missed Catalina; he really seemed in a bad way although he had no temperature. He refused his food and tugged at one of his ears, his face even more red and white than usual. The worst thing was the constant crying and Bernard being annoyed about it when he returned home. I had not been able to do much about an evening meal because I'd had the baby in my arms most of the time. It wasn't so much the flabby ham and boring undressed salad but the child's crying that got on his nerves.

We had a bit of an argument because I hadn't sent for the doctor; but he had had these crying fits before. Finally I took the screaming baby up to my room after Bernard had reproached me with "And we both thought you were so good with children." I stayed upstairs until Catalina returned; even then he was crying on and off until midnight when he fell into an exhausted sleep and so did I. At about six o'clock in the morning Catalina burst into my room with a smiling Johnny in her arms to show me that he had cut his third tooth. I hoped he never had another while I was around.

Besides being tired I was sulky with Bernard when he drove us to Twickenham; but Marline chattered away and I didn't think he noticed my mood. But in the evening when he came to fetch us he was very contrite and showered me with presents—a record of James Galway playing Bach and a box of marrons glacés, my favourite sweets, and also a ticket for a play at the Richmond Theatre I very much wanted to see, but it was a great success and I hadn't had time to queue for a ticket. He had another in his hand and said: "I know I don't deserve to, but can I come with you?" Of course I laughed and agreed and he was completely forgiven.

Bernard held me to him for a few moments and suddenly I felt a wave of love and closeness envelop me. I think Bernard must have felt a shadow of it because he looked quite startled, held me closer for a little time, then pushed me away and said something about hurrying if we were going to the theatre. I sailed up the narrow stairs, I can't remember walking, and sank into a dark velvet chair, a recent acquisition. I felt as if I were singing inside and there seemed to be a queer white light in the room. I stayed quite still until Tommy-Marline put her little face round the door and said, "Haven't you changed your clothes yet? Bernard's waiting for you," in a shocked way. Usually we never kept him waiting. I quickly changed, hardly knowing what I put on because I knew that whatever I wore that evening I should appear beautiful because I was shimmering with loving beauty. Bernard immediately noticed it and asked what I'd done to myself: "Why Bella! You look really charming in that dress. I've never seen it before." I smiled because I'd worn it all the previous summer.

We sat in the theatre, Bernard enthralled by Peter Barkworth's acting and me enthralled by Bernard. Sitting so close to him in the rather cramped seats was such a beautiful thing and even in the comparative darkness I could admire his haughty profile, rather like a hornbill's.

When we returned to Bernard's house we had a drink together sitting by the fire. Bernard wanted to discuss the play but there was little I could say. Puzzled, he asked if I was still annoyed with him, so I told him the truth, that I was quiet because I felt so happy, and he said, "How extraordinary, people so seldom admit they are happy. Gertrude did and look what happened to her. Take care, dear Bella. Happiness is a very fragile thing, but no one deserves it more than you."

Charlotte stayed away an extra week and when she returned she told us that she was engaged to be married to a German doctor. She was her old self again, high coloured and self-possessed, and had an argument with Bernard almost as soon as she entered the house. Then she upset Mrs. Hicks by giving her a large sausage highly fla-voured with garlic and suggested that they gave the house a good clean-up together. She frightened Johnny by kissing him when she was wearing a large felt hat and annoyed Catalina by making him cry. But if she did anything which might have annoyed me, I never noticed it because I was protected by my happiness. She did give me an unreadable German cookery book and I thanked her and said it was just what I'd always wanted, and I almost thought it was for a few minutes.

In spite of my love for Bernard I was glad to return to the freedom of the shop and to be queen of my own home—eat cornflakes or baked beans for supper, wear a dressing-gown for breakfast and read books that did not improve the mind in bed. There was a large box filled with second-hand ones in the shop, which I dipped into from time to time (so did my customers, often forgetting to pay the 20p). Tommy said, "I don't like living in two houses, mummy. There's no time to play," and she was right, we'd hardly had time to go in the Forbeses' beautiful garden during the last month. Another thing, Bernard was far more affectionate and open with me at the cottage than he was in his own house, perhaps because the memory of Gertrude was so strong it was as if she were with us. But that's how it was, he hardly ever touched me there.

The first evening at home I was alone except for Tommy, and after she went to bed I spent the evening telephoning my few friends and, of course, Mary Meadows. Mary had become quite worried in case I never returned to the shop and became absorbed by the Forbes family. I told her that was unlikely and how pleased I was to be home and how I hoped I'd be able to keep the shop open during August, but if business was very slack I'd spend the time collecting stock. Mary said it was almost as difficult to find stock as it was to sell it at that time of the year. She planned to drive round north east England to see what she could find and suggested I went with her. After a moment's hesitation I refused, partly because it wouldn't be much of a holiday for Tommy and might prove expensive, but mainly because I didn't want to be parted from Bernard.

He arrived early the following evening when Tommy and I were watering the garden and the tiny lawn was glistening. Tommy continued to water while we sat talking and drinking canned beer from glasses—neither of us liked drinking from the cans, anyway it wouldn't have suited Bernard's face. There was a little table placed between the white-painted garden chairs and we were not very close together although from time to time I did move my chair a little nearer. We were talking about Charlotte's coming marriage. It was to take place fairly soon and she was impatient to return to Germany, although she had reluctantly agreed to stay until someone suitable was found to take her place.

"Thank God we've got Catalina to care for Johnny. We don't want another of those battle-axe nannies," Bernard said dejectedly. "Couldn't you take it on, Bella? You are like one of the family already and I so hate all these strangers coming to the house and perhaps having to have meals with them." He held my bare arm with one of his beautifully-manicured hands (I'd moved much closer by this time) and pleaded with me to give up the shop and return permanently to Richmond: "I know I'm selfish, but think what a good thing it would be for Marlinchen—no more nurseries and playschools, she'd be brought up with Johnny as if she were his sister. It would have pleased Gertrude so much. Oh, Bella, do change your mind. It would be so good for all of us, including you, my dear girl."

I timidly put my hand over his and pleaded, "Please don't make me leave here, Bernard. I'm happier than I've ever been in my life, particularly on the days when I see you. I just fit in here and don't want to change anything. I'll do all I can to help you and Johnny, but let me stay here."

Bernard looked quite startled and exclaimed, "What a brute I must be, trying to change your life-style to suit my own ends! Of course you must stay here and be as happy as you like. But you'll still come for the weekends, won't you? It makes such a difference when you're there."

He left when it was growing dark but we didn't sit close again that evening. He just patted my head as if I were a good dog when we said goodnight.

19

WHEN MY mother heard that I'd been living in Bernard's house for over a month she was displeased that I hadn't asked her there although I explained that I'd been working in the shop all day and had been too busy to think of entertaining in someone else's house. "What about the weekends and the evenings?" she snapped down the telephone. "You have already told me that you cook a meal for the family every night; surely you could have had us one evening. I suppose you think that Bernard of yours will marry you. Well, I can assure you he won't. Can you imagine a man like that taking on a little black stepdaughter, not that she hasn't a certain charm, poor little mite. I must say I was very surprised to see how fond of her he appeared to be, but as for taking her into his family, that's another matter."

I said, "Mother, I do wish you wouldn't talk such nonsense. Bernard has no intention of marrying me or anyone else. He still worships Gertrude and always will and he would have married her if she had had ten black children. He has no feeling about colour whatever and Gertrude was the same."

Mother snorted. "So you think. I can't talk any longer, there's Mr. Crimony's supper to prepare—liver and bacon with mashed potatoes; but I suppose you despise that kind of meal."

I could almost smell the liver and bacon coming through the telephone wires until she crashed down the receiver in her usual rough way and we lost contact. I wondered why on earth she thought I should have asked her to Bernard's house. I had no idea she was so interested in him or his home. He must have made a great impression on her the only time they met, almost a year ago. All the same I seemed to remember her speaking to him in a very scathing way.

Charlotte had advertised in *The Times* for a lady cook-housekeeper and, to her surprise, there were twenty-seven replies: so we spent the weekend sorting through them. Most of the applicants seemed to be widows or divorcees, with or without children. Bernard said, "I don't think we want any extra children, we already have two. What about one of the young Spanish señoritas, they'd be company for Catalina?" But Charlotte thought the señoritas sounded rather frivolous, and there was the language difficulty. Her choice was a spinster of fifty-five, with good references and a small dog, and I favoured the eldest señorita, a girl of twenty-four. She seemed sympathetic and reliable and, if her letter was anything to go by, spoke good English. I was also interested in a childless divorcee of thirty-one, an out-of-work bookseller who wrote an excellent letter and didn't feel sorry for herself like most of the applicants, with their dead husbands and shattered marriages. By Monday we still hadn't made a final choice and I left it to the two of them to sort it out.

On Tuesday evening Bernard called, as he so often did, on his way home. He was later than usual and appeared depressed about the housekeeper Charlotte had chosen. "She is so obstinate, nothing will change her mind. She insists on the spinster with the small dog and good references. She's in Devonshire at the moment looking after the house of some old lady who has just died. Charlotte has already been on the phone to her. They were clacking away together when I left this morning and she says she will be free in about a week. Really, Bella, I dread her coming. Fifty-five is too old. She'll be set in her ways and want a nap in the afternoon and be no good at all with Johnny. I'd much rather have one of the Spanish girls; the older one you chose would be ideal."

He really looked worried so I suggested having the woman on a month's trial; then it would be much easier getting rid of her if necessary. He leapt from his chair: "That's a marvellous idea. Why didn't I think of it myself? I'll go home immediately and tell Charlotte all housekeepers must be on a month's trial. I can stand anything for a month, at least I think I can." He dashed from the house after only staying for about ten minutes. I wished I'd reserved my suggestion until later in the evening.

Charlotte had her own way and engaged the housekeeper of her choice—Joan Webb, she was called—but at least she was on a month's trial, so Bernard wasn't too committed. I didn't visit the house the first weekend she was there because I thought it rather unfair to burden her with extra people as soon as she arrived, but I went the following one because Charlotte had called at the shop—actually for the first time—and begged me to use my influence with Bernard to make him see what a nice little woman Joan Webb was. "I must admit she appears older than she said, fifty-five wasn't it? Otherwise she is a hardworking little soul, very bright and wanting to help. Unfortunately she's not very strong, can't drive the car and finds it difficult to carry the shopping up the hill; but Catalina has been helping, so there's not too much of a problem. Bernard says she has a certain arch brightness that appals him and he can't stand having meals with her. She's a bit of a fusser, I'm afraid, and so is the dog, always jumping up and down. He's called Fizz, and Bernard does not like that either."

I said, "I'm sorry to interrupt, but can she cook? That's one of the main things, isn't it?"

Charlotte looked surprised. "I suppose so. He hasn't complained about it much, although I must admit the helpings are very small. She goes in for egg dishes—fluffy omelettes, scrambled and poached eggs —and for meat there are tiny rissoles and sometimes minced meat in quite a nice sauce, and she does minced chicken too. I must say she's weak on vegetables and she forgets to buy cheese, thinks it indigestible perhaps. She likes cooking little tarts, but they are always the same— gooseberry. The old lady who died was very fond of them, it seems, but Bernard isn't. I don't know how she would manage a dinner party. But need there be dinner parties? He could entertain in his club, many men do. Anyway, the food doesn't seem to be the main issue; it's her twittering. Poor little woman! She is only trying to be friendly. And then in the evening she used scent and he told her to stop it because it gave him hay fever. What nonsense! It quite upset the poor woman.

I'm sure she is worth her weight in gold, what you'd call a treasure, if only Bernard would see it. You will do your best to influence him, won't you, Bella, dear?" And she was off without even glancing round the shop, all filled with minor treasures, and the morning sun streaming in through the windows on to the Bristol glass.

Bernard came to collect us on Saturday evening and said he could hardly bear to go home with that woman in the house. "She's got this small dog called Fizz that jumps about and quivers all the time. You can hardly tell the difference between them, they both have curly blue-grey hair. I hope you have eaten well today because you won't in my house. You'll be lucky if you get some watered-down tinned soup, followed by a broken poached egg, followed by a cup of weak tea or even cocoa."

We didn't drive off immediately, but sat in the car watching the cricket until Tommy said in a bored little voice, "When are we going to see the jumping dog?"

Bernard groaned: "Oh dear, she is going to be a Fizz fan." But he was smiling when we drove away.

As soon as Tommy reached the Forbeses' house and became Marline, she ignored her friend the carved bear and ran into the house to find the jumping dog and unearthed him in the kitchen, where Miss Webb was preparing the evening meal. For once he was lying under the table as Petra used to lie, but as soon as he heard our voices he leapt out from under the table with a burst ball in his mouth and raced round the room with Marline in pursuit. Bernard introduced me to Joan Webb, who said: "Do call me Joan, or Gay as my friends call me—they say I'm not in the least like a Joan. What do you think?" I said I thought both names were nice, then went upstairs to see Johnny who gave me a loving welcome. He was sitting in his high chair being fed by Catalina, who opened her mouth each time she put the spoon in Johnny's. Bernard took the spoon from Catalina and tried feeding the baby himself; but it wasn't a great success and he handed back the spoon and stood looking down at his son with an expression of great love and pride on his handsome face, an expression I had often seen when he was watching Gertrude.

We sat in the drawing-room waiting for dinner, Charlotte looking every now and then at her engagement ring and bringing her lover's name into the conversation whenever possible. She was obviously longing to return to Germany to join her Hermann. I was wondering if I ought to offer to help in the kitchen when Joan Webb came tripping in to announce dinner, with Fizz darting behind with the burst red ball protruding from his lips like an overgrown tongue. We trooped into the dining-room and were served with semolina cooked in a milky cheese sauce, followed by trifle smothered in a custard powder sauce and decorated with hundreds and thousands. We sat quietly eating our baby-food while Joan tried to make polite conversation: "Oh! Mr. Forbes, I only heard today that you are partial to steaks. I thought you were more or less a vegetarian, but tomorrow you shall have your steak. Oh dear! Tomorrow is Sunday and the shops will be closed and I'd planned minced chicken. Never mind. Monday will be a steak day and even Fizz will have a tiny slice." And Fizz, who had settled down, started leaping and quivering round the table with a fearful alert look in his eyes.

On Sunday morning when Bernard had shut himself in his study with the *Sunday Times* and Charlotte was sitting on the lawn reading *The Observer* and Catalina had taken the children to the park, I went into the kitchen to help Miss Webb in any way I could. Although she was unsuitable I felt sorry for the poor little woman. Charlotte appeared to have left her to her own devices without any helpful advice or guidance. I managed to gain her confidence as we washed up the breakfast things together and it was obvious she was far from happy. I went through the larder and kitchen cupboards with her and could find no Forbes-like food lurking there. There was an anaemic-looking chicken already cooked and waiting to be minced, a heartless lettuce, dark green cabbage, a floppy pink blancmange, many packets of soup, dried vegetables and mashed potato and, of course, tins of gooseberries. The pink blancmange was obviously the pride of the collection and I had to be cruel and dismiss it as "perhaps something the children will eat." In its place I suggested a fresh fruit salad and whipped cream. Her face crumpled: "They don't like blancmange! I can hardly believe it. My mother enjoyed it until the day she died, (poor soul, she was ninety) and all the ladies I have worked for have been devoted to it. I'm afraid the trouble is I've only cooked for the elderly and never for a man." I left her slicing onions with tears streaming down her powdered cheeks. I hoped they were caused by the onions.

I hurried to the nearest Indian shop that was open and bought peppers, red and green, a shining dark aubergine and some peaches, oranges and bananas and a large carton of cream. When I returned I put the chicken, peppers and aubergine into a casserole and, to Joan Webb's horror, added some of the dried mushrooms and garlic hanging from the ceiling, also a glass of sherry (Bernard's best). We prepared the fresh fruit salad together and beat the cream and I stopped her little hand reaching out for a packet of dehydrated mashed potato and suggested rice instead. Then we had a late cup of coffee together and she opened up her heart. She told me how she had refused two proposals of marriage and stayed at home to look after her mother who had a pension and a comfortable annuity so money had been no problem. Indeed, "mummy" had insisted on her only daughter dressing well. She liked to see her in pretty clothes, blue for preference, to match her blue eyes. And until the last few years she had encouraged her to go out with her friends, though of course this changed when "mummy" became almost helpless.

"When she died, it was a shock about the money. It all stopped—pension, annuity, all of it. There was about £700 in the bank, but the funeral cost much more than I expected. I sold the furniture, but it didn't fetch much, although mummy had such good taste. Then there was Fizz to look after. Mummy's dear dog. I couldn't have him put down. It was a close friend, our lawyer, who suggested I took a post as cook-housekeeper to an elderly lady. You see I'd had so much experience with mummy all those years, it was the only thing I could do. It worked beautifully. I was very happy with my old ladies. One was a bit of a tartar, she even tried to bite my hand when I was feeding her and eventually had to be placed in a home: but the others were dears except that they were inclined to die. I lost three of them in four years. That's why I answered Mr. Forbes's advertisement—a widower with a baby son sounded so hopeful. Of course, I'd no idea how large the house was, and situated on a steep hill too. There's no one to advise me about my work either. Miss Charlotte only cares about returning to Germany and her coming marriage and Mr. Forbes hardly speaks to me if he can help it, although I do try and make a little cheerful conversation." She put down her coffee cup and said in a low voice. "Another thing that worries me is the money."

Surprised, I exclaimed: "Don't they give you enough?"

She shook her head thoughtfully. "I don't know. You see Miss Charlotte gave me two hundred pounds, to pay for the food, she said; but she didn't say how long it had to last and already I've spent thirty pounds in two weeks. The milk comes to quite a lot and the Spanish nanny has a large appetite, always munching French loaves filled with sausage, tomatoes and onions. I couldn't do it myself, but she's a hard-working girl and needs it, she says. I have tried to talk to Mr. Forbes, but he's a difficult man to talk to, isn't he?"

I told her I'd speak to him and she wasn't to worry because she certainly hadn't spent too much money, in fact, she'd spent too little.

We could hear Bernard calling for me so I said, "Take care you don't over-cook the rice, the grains should stay separate," and skimmed away to him. He wanted to show me some yellow poppies he'd recently found growing in Gertrude's thicket under an apple tree among a tangle of long grass. Neither of us had seen them before, although they looked well established, and it was as if they were a message of hope from Gertrude. We both felt this.

Bernard said, "I wouldn't be surprised if they were gone tomorrow, they don't seem real somehow."

They were fragile flowers, but real enough and I thought it likely that they'd still be there tomorrow. We carefully searched the thicket but found no more yellow poppies.

After lunch, when we were sitting in the drawing-room drinking our coffee, Charlotte said: "That was a very good meal Joan gave us. I said she would turn out to be a treasure, it's just a matter of settling down." Bernard looked thoughtful, then asked me where I'd been most of the morning. Had I been hiding in the kitchen by any chance?

I thought it a good time to tell them exactly what had been going on in the kitchen, the pathetic money problem and lack of guidance and instructions, Joan's sad little history, not tragic, but really sad. Her old ladies dying one by one, three lost in four years, and her cooking based on the needs of the impoverished and elderly.

Charlotte said crossly: "How was I supposed to know all that. She said she was an experienced cook and I left her to get on with it. After all, I shan't be here much longer so it's no good her depending on me. She did say something about the money and I told her to ask Bernard. The two hundred was supposed to cover her salary for a month and the shopping, perhaps I didn't make it clear. Now I come to think of it, I don't know what her salary is, do you, Bernard?"

"No," he said crossly. "You made all the arrangements. You've been thoroughly irresponsible," and he banged down his coffee cup and left the room.

Charlotte turned to me and said, "Now look what you have done. I asked you to help, not interfere."

20

JOAN WEBB, or Gay, as she wished to be called, stayed on for nearly three more weeks, then left to look after an ancient lady who had a flat in nearby Ham. Her cooking did improve a little, with help from Charlotte, but she found the house too large and the hill too steep, Johnny too heavy and Bernard disconcerting. Altogether she found the Forbeses' house a very frightening place. She was to get a much smaller salary in this new job but she said she didn't mind. It was a home she wanted and her pension would start in a few months. She had been so looking forward to her pension, she said, quite forgetting she was supposed to be fifty-five, not fifty-nine.

Bernard gradually grew less hostile to her, particularly when he knew she was leaving, but he never took to poor Fizz, who continued to leap on to the backs of sofas, sometimes landing on Bernard's head. He pranced and quivered, barked and whined, and had this fearfully eager expression. One of his eyes had a queer blue-green glint which made him look as if he were wearing a monocle.

Bernard drove the dog and his mistress to their new home, Fizz sitting on the luggage in the back of the Volvo, barking all the way. "I was glad to see the last of them," Bernard said later as he sat in his chair in the room behind the shop. "The poor old lady did improve a little but she was always so skittish with me, right until the end; nerves, I suppose. She used to bring out those bright little observations like slightly soiled visiting cards. She had one for every occasion. Did you know Charlotte has relented about the señoritas and one is coming from an agency next week? There will be none of that nonsense of having meals together. The two girls will eat in the kitchen at a time that suits them and live on Spanish food for all I care. I rather like it myself but don't want it every day."

He left his chair and stood beside me and I hoped he'd touch me, but he didn't immediately, he went on talking about domestic things. "Charlotte is giving this new girl a week, then she's off. This engagement seems to have upset her and she acts quite out of character. I'll be glad when I've settled down with Johnny and the two señoritas and things are more or less normal, as normal as they will ever be." Then he put his arms around me and said, "You know, you are the dearest girl. I don't know how I would manage without you."

We stayed like that, close together, for some time and I wished it could have been for ever. When he was leaving, I asked, "Are the yellow poppies still there?"

Surprised, he exclaimed, "Good Lord! I haven't looked. I'd forgotten all about them." Then he went away. I didn't see him out of the house as I usually did, but stood quite still, thinking. Was Bernard very slightly forgetting Gertrude?

When August came I closed the shop for a fortnight, as I had the previous year. I spent the first week at Richmond, partly for my daughter's sake and partly to help Charlotte, who was returning to Germany in a matter of days and was entangled in a tremendous amount of shopping and packing. We were friends again, although I didn't really care for her much. She was far too bossy and self-centred. The Spanish cook-housekeeper was now installed and the house was more noisy than it used to be, with the two girls shouting to each other up and down the stairs and harsh voices and laughter coming from the kitchen. The new girl was called Isabel and she was several years older than Catalina and had a Spanish *novio*—a waiter. The two girls worked well together and Isabel was always ready to give a helping hand with Johnny and looked after him completely on Catalina's day off. Charlotte and I wrote out a list of suitable meals to serve to Bernard and hung it up in the kitchen and it seemed to work out quite well, although he occasionally complained that too much frying was going on.

It was very different to last year's visit, when Gertrude and I had been so happy together sitting under the juniper tree and eating delicious picnics in our Burning Bush Restaurant, with the magpies overhead watching us with their clever eyes and the cock bird sometimes coming down and helping himself to the most unexpected morsels of food, smoked salmon and ham or, to our dismay, chicken if he got the chance, which seemed like cannibalism to us. Now I used to sit there by myself, just to be quiet, really. There were still a few yellow poppies under the apple tree and I'd identified them from one of Gertrude's botany books and learnt that they were called *Meconopsis cambrica* and were natives of the mountains of western Europe, but sometimes found in valleys.

I spent the second week's holiday at home with Tommy. I redecorated the shop with Mary Meadow's help and so enjoyed her company. We took Tommy to Chessington Zoo and she fell in love with an orang-outan with a most compelling personality and a look of great wisdom. Mary said, "He reminds me of Bernard," which slightly annoyed me because I could see what she meant. On fine days I sometimes took Tommy for bicycle rides sitting in her little seat behind me. We had picnics in the local parks and a favourite place—Teddington Lock.

I used to look forward to Stephen's letters from New York; but now I put them on the mantelshelf and forgot them for several days. I was thinking of Bernard all the time. I loved him so much, but was content as long as I saw him two or three times a week and we sometimes touched each other or sat very close. Of course, he didn't feel like this about me, but he was fond of me and my presence seemed to give him some sort of comfort: also he felt that I was partly his creation, that he had moulded me. This was true, he and Gertrude had both moulded me, Gertrude unconsciously. In a book of D. H. Lawrence's poems they had given me I came on these lines:

"And how I am not all except a flame that mounts off you
Where I touch you, I flame into being: but is it me or you?"

That is how I felt for Bernard, as if he were a flame. But I wasn't a flame to him.

It was a long time since I'd seen my mother and our only communication had been the harsh telephone conversations we sometimes had. Then she arrived in her red Rover one Saturday afternoon towards the end of summer. She was accompanied by her shadow, Mr. Crimony, carrying parcels that could be presents. Tommy ran to the shop window crying, "Mister Chimney is coming with lots of presents, quick, open the door!" I was wrapping up some Crown Derby plates a customer had just bought, so I told Tommy to open the door herself. She flung her arms round Mr. Crimony's legs, ignoring my mother, which upset her and put a strain on the visit which took a little time to wear off.

The presents consisted of a large fluffy cream cake, a large fluffy toy dog for Tommy and a fuchsia in a pot for me. Tommy was delighted with the rather vulgar toy and said it was exactly like Fizz and that was to be his name.

Mother snapped, "That's a silly name for a silly dog. I can't think why you waste your money on such rubbish, Charlie." Then, half way through tea, when we were all sticky from the sweet cream cake, she produced an envelope from her bag and gave it to Tommy.

She tore it open, then said sadly, "But it's only a little book without pictures," and handed me a small blue post office savings book. There was only one entry but it was for a hundred pounds, a handsome sum for a child to start a savings account with. I repeatedly thanked my mother, but Tommy wasn't impressed and much preferred the fluffy dog, which pleased Mr. Crimony.

After tea we sat in the garden because it was inclined to be dark in the room behind the shop and there seemed to be too many people in it. This year I'd planted a lot of snap dragons I'd grown from seed and the roses had done well, particularly a climbing white one that smelt very sweet, but all mother could see was the buses dashing past, only the tops of them over the tall gate, and they made a wooshing sound like sea waves and the lorries a sound like lions roaring—I'd grown used to the noise. Mother still had her job in the travel agency and offered to arrange a cheap off-season holiday for me; but I had already had my holiday and didn't want another.

Mr. Crimony and Tommy took fluffy Fizz for a walk on the Green, frequently stopping by trees so that he could lift his leg as she had seen the real Fizz do. When we were alone mother immediately started to ask questions about Bernard. I told her about Joan Webb because I thought it would amuse her; but she was quite shocked to hear that he was now living alone with two señoritas. "Good-looking girls, you say. Catholics, I suppose, so at least he won't be able to marry one of them without a lot of trouble. Do you see him often? However much he loved his wife, I don't think he will stay a widower for long. Such a handsome man, and wealthy too. Oh, you say he is coming this evening? Why didn't you tell me before?"

Mother hung about as long as she could, hoping to see how we behaved towards each other, but Mr. Crimony started fretting for his supper. There were herrings waiting in the fridge at home: "You can't expect me to eat them in the middle of the night. That's asking for indigestion," he said petulantly. So they drove away in the red Rover; but still Bernard didn't come.

At about eight he phoned to say he was on his way. He had been delayed by a domestic crisis, but would be with us as quickly as possible. By this time Tommy had fallen asleep in a chair, still clutching her vulgar dog. When Bernard did arrive, he appeared very distraught and bundled us into the car, laying Tommy, who was still asleep, on the back seat. He said crossly, "Isabel has gone, so there won't be a meal waiting unless Catalina has prepared something. I'll tell you about it when we get home."

I said regretfully, "Things seemed to be working so well with the two girls," and we didn't speak again until we reached Richmond. It was as if we were breathing tired air.

When we entered the house I hurried upstairs with Marline in my arms and put her to bed without washing her and she still had some of her clothes on, but she was so deeply sleeping I didn't want to disturb her. She was still clutching the fluffy dog. When I went downstairs Bernard was waiting for me in the hall and we walked into the drawing-room together. The room was in disorder and there was a strong smell of cigarette smoke combined with stale wine, although one of the windows was open. Then I saw the overflowing ashtrays and a half-empty bottle standing on the inlaid rosewood table and another lying empty on its side in a little pool of dark wine. Bernard said, "Disgusting, isn't it? I came home early and that's what I found. There were three men, one of them a waiter I'd seen here before, and Isabel, all of them sitting round the table playing cards and drinking my precious Château Lafite-Rothschild 1962. The waiter was fully dressed in his waiter's clothes but the other two had their shirts and ties hanging over the back of their chairs and were wearing vests. There they were, sitting in Gertrude's drawing-room in their revolting vests. I told them to leave the house immediately and, I must admit, they gave me no trouble, one even apologized for entering the house uninvited. It was Isabel who was really troublesome, screaming at me in Spanish, then practically having hysterics, while the two men quietly dressed, bowed politely and left the house. It was like some horrible film."

I interrupted, "But where's Catalina? She hasn't gone too, has she?"

Bernard looked bewildered. "I suppose she's still in her room. I sent her up there when Isabel was trying to make her leave the house with her and poor Johnny was screaming his head off and the women shouting above it. The waiter boyfriend did his best to calm them, eventually escorting Catalina and the child from the room, giving them little pats as he did so as if they were dogs. It took about an hour to get Isabel out of the house and she had to be practically carried to the boyfriend's car, but when she was safely shut in, the man turned to me and said coolly he was sorry about the wine but he'd replace it as soon as possible, and we parted on quite good terms."

I went into the kitchen to prepare a simple meal of some kind and found Catalina wearing a tragic tearstained face. She ran to me like a child and sobbed in my arms, then we went to the drawing-room and opened the french windows wide to the evening air and gave the room a quick clean and mopped at the wine-stained carpet. Within an hour the three of us were eating an omelette and an appetizing salad in the kitchen. We finished off the wine too. Bernard said it was a fabulous French one that he gave to very special art dealers and was not meant to be drunk in the kitchen and he looked round with interest. I think it was the first time he had eaten in his kitchen.

21

ON MONDAY morning Bernard and I went to Mrs. Vic's domestic agency, but after waiting for a few minutes he said he was very busy at the gallery and disappeared, and I was left to face Mrs. Vic alone. She was an elderly woman with piled-up white hair and a very straight back. As I was talking to her I found I was straightening mine. In time I became quite at home at Mrs. Vic's, but I found that first visit rather intimidating. She kept trying to make me accept young mothers with one or two children and I knew Bernard was very against this. He said he didn't want the house turned into a crèche and he didn't want any pets either.

In the afternoon four women called about the job, some overlapping. The most attractive applicant had a small son of four dressed in red. He was a lively child and ran round and round the lawn until his bright brown hair became wet with sweat, then worked the gentle swing up to such a pitch that he was in danger of going over the top. Bernard would never have stood him; but I was sorry to see them go because I knew they lived in a cramped bedsitting-room.

There was a handsome Spanish girl, very like Isabel, but I felt we didn't want any more señoritas for the time being. We needed someone rather stodgy.

The last two were both experienced cook-housekeepers and they had references to prove it. They were both around forty-five and had good figures and dull faces, but there was one difference; one was a spinster and the other divorced. The spinster was free to start work immediately, so I chose her, although her round face had a slightly spiteful expression, and on the whole it wasn't a bad choice.

Her name was May Jones and she was always known as Miss May and, to the children, Missy May. I stayed for a week to settle her in, and she wasn't difficult to settle, then I left her to Bernard. He had no complaints except that she wasn't very good with Johnny, and I often had to spend my free Mondays with him when Catalina met her friends in London.

One funny thing happened soon after Miss May arrived. Isabel's *novio* the waiter called at the house one afternoon with two bottles of Château Lafite-Rothschild 1962 for Bernard. We could hardly believe it. But it was really an excuse to see Catalina again. Isabel was forgotten and they became serious *novios* and in her spare time Catalina embroidered initials on double sheets and flower-decorated towels of all sizes.

Early in October I began to ponder about Johnny's birthday on the ninth. It should be a happy day for the little boy although it was the first anniversary of his mother's death and would be a terrible day for his father. I bought him a handmade engine of brightly decorated wood, which he would be able to pull about in a month or two's time. He was already standing but preferred crawling to walking. Summoning my courage, I showed Bernard the toy engine, half expecting him to pounce on me for being interfering; but he was grateful to me for mentioning the subject and said he needed my help. So on the Monday before the ninth we went to Harrods' toy department together and rather enjoyed ourselves, though I had to restrain Bernard from buying the most unsuitable presents for a boy of one year—tricycles and bicycles and construction sets, for boys of at least ten. I had to steer him towards teddy bears and musical boxes and multi-coloured balls. Bernard chose a very large teddy bear (quite a bit larger than Johnny and too big for him to play with, but I hadn't the heart to say this), a very decorative hobby horse, a spinning top, balls of all sizes and, as we were leaving, a large jumping frog.

From Harrods we went to Bernard's gallery, a slightly awesome place where people spoke in soft voices. From the street one saw only one dark painting in the window, a painting of dark, sorrowing figures of long ago, but inside, in the main gallery, there were some arresting

Spanish paintings by Antonio Clavé and two small Mirós and, what pleased me very much, a painting by Tàpies, an artist that Bernard had taught me to love and understand. While Bernard conducted his business a good-looking assistant wearing a beautiful suit stood talking to me. I had met him several times in the gallery and once at Richmond and he never seemed quite real to me, but I liked him in a superficial way. Bernard was in a cheerful mood and, when his business was finished, took me out to lunch. Over lunch he told me that he had decided I was to learn to speak French properly. French was one of the few things I'd learnt from my mother, but hers was much better than mine and I could only speak in a stilted way. It was arranged that a French woman was to call at the shop two evenings a week and the course was to be very thorough, but, as a reward when it was finished, Bernard would take me to Brussels to see the gallery he was buying a partnership in. He said he wanted me to see it so that we could talk about it together and that it would mean something to me. In fact, I could go there quite often if I was interested. My chatter would keep him awake when he was driving.

Johnny's birthday was all I hoped it would be and Bernard was there for the cutting of the cake and main present-giving. Miss May had made the cake and, of course, came to the tea. I was pleased to see how well she fitted in—she treated Bernard in a friendly but impersonal way which suited him. The presents were unwrapped by Marline and handed to Johnny, who was delighted with everything, including the crumpled paper wrappings, although he didn't know what they were, but the present he liked best was a small mechanical bird that fluttered its wings and pecked the ground when wound up—a present from Marline. Naturally he didn't quite understand about blowing the candles out, so Marline helped him with that too. When the tea was over, Bernard carried him round the nursery showing him the presents and helping him stand on his strong feet. Actually I think he gave his first steps that day. It was difficult to see because it was over so quickly, but Bernard always said he did.

After the birthday party he drove us home and, when I'd put my sleepy daughter to bed, he asked if he could stay for the evening and settled down in his chair in the odd little room behind the shop while I prepared a simple meal of mushrooms on toast and cheese and fruit. The few bottles of wine in the cottage were provided by Bernard so I told him to choose his own bottle and open it before I made the toast so that we could drink and talk a little before eating.

At first we talked of Brussels and the new gallery partnership. Then, while we were eating, we talked of Johnny and what a splendid child he was and how Gertrude would have loved him, and it was as if she had crept into the room. He talked about her great beauty and intelligence and how everyone had loved her, how extraordinarily graceful, and all her movements so perfect. "Do you remember the way she used to slowly turn her head and look at you with her great heavy-lidded eyes? Sometimes she was laughing—she loved to laugh, didn't she?"

By this time we were sitting very close and he was ruffling my hair with his long fingers and I pondered on something to say to change the conversation, if you could call it a conversation. Eventually I said: "Bernard, did you really mean I chatter?"

His mood changed and he laughed and stopped ruffling my hair. "No, of course I didn't, you are the mistress of *Bel-Gazou,* my dear."

I asked, "But what does *Bel-Gazou* mean?" and he said I'd know when I'd studied my French. Then we stood up and we kissed for the first time and went upstairs and, for the first time, lay on the bed together. Bernard was in my arms but I wasn't in his and we stayed like that until my arms grew stiff. The street lamps dimly lit the room and I could look at his beautiful, haughty profile for as long as I wanted and it was heaven to be touching him, but I wished Gertrude wasn't there. In real life she had never been in my bedroom.

At about six-thirty there was a great rumbling and hissing and the room was filled with flashing lights. Bernard, all startled, asked what was happening, so I told him it was only Flash Harry, a street-cleaning engine that passed every morning. He said, "We don't have things like that in Richmond as far as I know, but of course we sleep at the back." He kissed me on the forehead and said, "Goodbye, little *Bel-Gazou,*" and in moments of tenderness he continued to use that name.

22

AT THE end of October, when there was no warmth left in the sun, I heard that Miss Murray had suddenly died of peritonitis. It was Mary who told me and we were both shocked because it was she who had introduced us to each other. She had been so kind in her reserved way, bringing me china when stocks were low and the helpful advice she had sometimes given me. Although I didn't see her often she had become part of my life, and then I'd met her on the same snowy day that I'd met Gertrude.

A few days after I'd heard of her death I received a letter from her lawyers saying that under the will of the late Edith Murray she had bequeathed to me the entire contents of her shop with the exception of three objects which were to go to her brother. It was just a matter of waiting for probate, it seemed. I couldn't believe the letter was true at first and re-read it before I telephoned Mary.

Mary was almost as pleased as I was and we made plans for collecting and storing the contents of the shop, but, to my surprise, Bernard was against me accepting the legacy; he thought everything should go to the brother. So I rather bravely telephoned the lawyers and said I was prepared to give up my claim to the contents of the shop if Miss Murray's brother felt bitter about it. The lawyer assured me that Mr. Murray had no interest in the shop whatever and had already taken away the three quite valuable pieces of furniture that had been specially willed to him, and now all he was waiting for was for the shop to be emptied so that he could hand over the lease. When I told Bernard this he seemed a little annoyed at first, but eventually he laughed and said that, if the brother didn't care about his sister's shop, it was perfectly right for me to accept it. Then he admitted that he'd felt a little jealous. He wanted any good fortune that came my way to have come from him. He appeared quite ashamed about this and turned his face away, so I said, "All I want is for us both to help each other as much as we possibly can," and for a moment our hands touched.

I was working hard at my French. My teacher was quite a young girl and not at all severe. Her English was good so she had no difficulty in explaining things to me and I enjoyed our French conversations. Lucie came twice a week and after the lesson she often stayed for a meal and we talked about our lives and loves and ambitions, sometimes in English and sometimes in French, and I could feel my French improving when I was talking naturally and it wasn't a lesson. Bernard came round one evening to see how I was progressing, but Lucie and I became self-conscious and the lesson wasn't a success. I wondered how good I'd have to be before Bernard took me to Brussels. I tried not to look forward to it too much but it was always there at the back of my mind, this magical journey with Bernard to a place where Gertrude had never been as far as I knew. Sometimes we would be travelling in the car and other times flying first class and drinking champagne and in my dreams we'd even be travelling by sledge, surrounded by snowy forests. Very occasionally we'd be voyaging by night in a small cargo boat and we'd walk on the empty dark decks with our arms round each other and, when we kissed, our lips would taste of sea spray. Actually, when we did go to Brussels, we made the short journey by air.

We really went earlier than we intended because of a looming domestic crisis. Catalina wanted to marry her waiter, so we had to go away together while we still had her to look after the children. We couldn't leave them in the charge of Miss May who made it quite clear that she was there to cook and housekeep and not to look after young children. She did occasionally take Johnny for a short walk in his pram and was known to babysit when he was deeply asleep, but she was really a little scared of children.

It was a Sunday morning when Catalina dropped her bombshell about getting married. In spite of all the sewing that had been going on we hadn't expected her to marry for a year at least and now she was hoping to have a Christmas wedding. She had offered to stay on after her marriage if Bernard didn't mind her husband living in the house. "He'd help at your dinner parties, Mister Bernard, and he's very good with electrical apparatus."

For a moment Bernard was speechless, then he said, "Yes, er—yes, I'm sure he would be most helpful; but I don't think it would quite work out, although I'll keep it in mind."

Catalina smiled. "Okay, Mister Bernard, you think about it. Not to worry," and she skipped from the room.

Bernard sank on to a sofa and said: "Where does she get her English? Not from this house, I hope." He pulled me down beside him and smoothed my bare arm with the tip of one finger and I felt as if I'd been touched by a rainbow, but it meant nothing to him, he only wanted my attention and advice. "Bella, you don't think I ought to have that man living in the house for Johnny's sake, do you? He'd be all over the place, in here, everywhere. He's so pushing, like a badly-trained dog. If he had a tail he'd be wagging it all the time. You've hardly seen him, Bella. But off duty he usually wears a brown plastic imitation-leather outfit, and his hair has been curled in some horrible way." He turned away and his fine nostrils appeared to quiver, though it may have been my imagination.

I said, "Bernard, don't torture yourself. Of course you needn't have that man living in the house. Why, he might even borrow your suits!"

"Fortunately they wouldn't fit," he said in a more relaxed way. "After all, there are about six weeks before Catalina leaves. Let's see what Mrs. Vic has to offer."

A day or two later Bernard came to the shop on his way home. I was standing on a stool reaching for something hanging high in the window and he stood outside watching me. When I'd finished he came in and lifted me off the stool, held me to him, then kissed me on the lips in a really loving way although the shop lights were shining brightly. We went into the back room where Tommy was sitting at the table eating her supper of apple pie and drinking milk through a whirly glass tube—this evening the milk was tinted pink.

Bernard kissed her on the top of her curly head and said, "If mummy has a little holiday with me, will you come to Richmond and help Catalina look after Johnny?"

Tommy blew the milk in reverse and said, "Of course, I always do."

That was the first I'd heard about going to Brussels so soon. Apparently Bernard had to meet several important people there the following week and had suddenly decided we should leave immediately. "And as for your French, your accent may be individual, but you're amazingly fluent." He then insisted on giving me a cheque for a hundred pounds to buy anything I needed, a dress perhaps. "These people in Brussels are really rather formal and will expect you as my protégée to be well dressed. I hope they won't bore you."

With all the excitement I became quite emotional and said, "Dear Bernard, I can never be bored if you are there."

We left the following Tuesday and, although the journey wasn't quite like my dreams, it was very pleasant flying first class and sitting close to Bernard as he worked, not very seriously, planning out an itinerary for our visit which would only last five days. Part of the time I was to be in the care of a secretary who would take me to museums and galleries while Bernard attended to his really serious business.

The five days passed so quickly, not the nights, but the days. I was introduced to people as Bernard's protégée and they appeared to like me. It was one of those times when I was looking beautiful with happiness and I think they felt this radiance glowing from me and it made them happy too. It was the same at parties: everyone seemed to want to talk to me and there I'd stand, almost like a queen bee, with Bernard by my side; but it was the nights that were so perfect, at least almost perfect. Even in bed Bernard had a certain reserve and in our relationship it was always like that. I must never be the one to make the first advances—answer his passion, but never make the first move. That was how he wanted it and anything he wanted was perfect to me. Just to be with him was the purest happiness. When we left our hotel bedroom for the last time, I said, "Bernard, how Women's Lib would hate me if they knew how I felt about you."

23

IN BRUSSELS we had really left Gertrude behind, there wasn't the faintest shadow of her, but when we returned to England her gentle presence was waiting, or so it seemed to me. Bernard would say: "I don't think Gertrude would approve of those playsuits Johnny is wearing. They make him look like a mechanic," or to Miss May: "I'd rather you didn't serve boiled cod, Miss May. My wife dislikes it." Mrs. Hicks would be asked to change the curtains in "the mistress's bed-room" or even to take "the mistress's dressing-gown to the cleaners." The soft blue dressing-gown hung on a hook on the door; but Ger-trude's other clothes nestled in the large cupboards that had drawers as well as hanging rails and her jewel-case was locked away somewhere. Mrs. Hicks and I had been greatly daring and cleared the dressing-table of Gertrude's simple but expensive cosmetics. We kept them for a month in a kitchen drawer, then, as Bernard did not appear to miss them, Mrs. Hicks took them home to her young daughter, who said they were "wishy-washy" and threw them in the dustbin.

One of the first things I did on my return was to pay a visit to Mrs. Vic's agency. I brought back a list of five would-be nurses for Johnny. There was the usual elderly nanny, the untrained girl with a baby of her own, and three experienced girls who sounded quite promising; one of them was Dutch which I thought might appeal to Bernard. But in the evening when I showed him the list, he glanced at it and said they wouldn't do. Gertrude wouldn't approve of them. Then he asked me to do the one thing I couldn't bring myself to do even for Bernard, give up the shop and look after the Forbes family and house. We had quite an argument about this, which ended in Bernard admitting that he was a selfish brute, then staying the night with me. It was almost as it had been in Brussels, but not quite, because I felt a selfish brute myself and hoped I had the strength of will to stay one.

After all, Bernard chose the Dutch girl to look after Johnny. She was called Greta and spoke perfect English so the poor child didn't have to learn a third language—as it was he spoke more Spanish than anything, but his vocabulary was still very limited. For nearly a fortnight he was cared for by two doting nurses; then Catalina left for Spain with her *novio* and Johnny was alone with Greta and he didn't like it at all. Marline and I were the only ones who could comfort him. He would go to Bernard for a few minutes, but then his bottom lip would quiver and he'd hold his arms out to me. I spent all the time I could with him, but didn't want to neglect the shop too much, particularly as it was nearly Christmas, my busy time. Gradually Johnny settled down with Greta and his relationship with his father improved. Bernard spent as much time as he could with him, which meant that he seldom called on me on his way home. Marline and I still spent Sunday and most of Monday at the Richmond house and I enjoyed it in a way, the luxury and long talks with Bernard, but we never came close to each other there. Bernard seemed to edge away if I came the slightest bit close.

A strange thing happened in the early spring. Bernard's gold cuff-links disappeared from the dressing-table. They had been lying there for several days while he wore some Victorian ones I'd given him for Christmas; then suddenly the gold ones vanished. Nothing else was missing. At first we thought Mrs. Hicks or Miss May had flicked them to the floor with the feather duster they were fond of using, so the furniture was moved and the floor searched, then the insides of the carpet sweeper and the repulsive bag of dust, but all we found were pins and paper clips. As nothing else vanished in mysterious circumstances the cuff-links were almost forgotten until I found one under the juniper tree in Gertrude's wild garden. I often sat there on the low bench now the weather was warmer and I'd been there the previous day; but there hadn't been the slightest glitter of gold in the spring sun and now it was shining on something gold hanging from a twig like a Christmas tree decoration, Bernard's cuff-link. I took it down and examined it closely, but it was quite unharmed; then I searched for its companion, but there was no more shining gold, only the magpies chattering high in the cherry tree near their domed nest. When I showed Bernard my find, he was all for climbing a ladder to hunt for the other link in the magpies' nest. But for once our positions were reversed; I said: "Gertrude wouldn't like her magpies disturbed at this time of the year, they might even fly away. Wait until the autumn," and he reluctantly agreed.

As time went on Bernard became more devoted to Johnny and Johnny to him, but also to Marline. The children only spent the weekends together and they made the most of it and sometimes Bernard felt a little neglected. But, on the other hand, so did I, neglected by Bernard.

Johnny's second birthday came and he was showered with expensive presents and blew out both candles on his birthday cake with one breath, which we all agreed was a good omen for the future. Three days later he bit Greta on the arm when they were having a bit of a tussle about something and she slapped him in return. I wasn't there at the time but Bernard was in the next room and came rushing in and from what he told me there was rather a nasty scene and Greta gave her notice. Bernard arrived quite late at night to tell me this. He said he hadn't liked to leave Johnny until he was sure he was soundly asleep. "Do you think she has been hitting him all the time and I didn't know?" he asked dejectedly. "I always thought they got on together quite well."

I said, "An occasional slap isn't the end of the world and biting is a nasty habit and should be checked. Greta is a little impersonal, but not a bad nurse. I think it a great pity she is leaving."

Bernard suddenly stood up and seemed to be towering above me. He almost shouted, "I'm no good at being a one-parent family and I won't put up with it any more. It isn't fair to Johnny, let alone me. Bella, you'll have to marry me."

No mention of love, just, "Bella, you'll have to marry me." I refused. Mary came round to the shop some days later and the two of us sat on some rather shaky Regency chairs, drinking instant coffee and talking about how impossible it was for me to marry Bernard. "You would lose everything if you did, your freedom, the shop and your individuality," Mary said with great emphasis, and I agreed. Tommy and I were as free as air, but if we lived with Bernard we would have to conform to his standards. I could never stay in bed late on Sunday mornings reading my horoscope in the *Sunday Express,* perhaps with Tommy curled up beside me. I'd have to drop some of my friends, the rather jolly antique dealers whom I sometimes had drinks with and the friendly customers who used to bring me flowers from their gardens, not important people, but kind. I told Mary how stiff Bernard was towards me in his own home. Would it always be like that if we lived there together? Would I have to be a permanent nurse to the rather spoilt Johnny and perhaps be cook-housekeeper as well? We could find no reason for marrying Bernard except the luxury of a bath every day. Even my deep love for him was a handicap because he didn't feel the same for me. Mary had come so that we could go over the shop's accounts together, but we didn't work very hard that morning. I was half laughing and half crying and figures had little meaning. I couldn't remember why the petty cash was so heavy in September or how much it had cost to replace a sofa's leg. I said, "Oh, Mary, he sometimes calls me *Bel-Gazou.*"

24

We woke with a start. Flash Harry was clanking and hissing and flashing coloured lights on the bedroom wall. Bernard said, "We'll miss him when you leave here. I've become quite fond of Flash Harry." Then he left our warm bed and quickly dressed in his perfect clothes, even brushing his suit in the darkness. He always returned to Richmond early because there were no proper toilet facilities in my little house.

I half sat up and said: "Bernard, what do you mean? I'm not leaving here?" and he said soothingly, "Go to sleep, my darling. We'll talk about it tomorrow," and I fell asleep again and couldn't quite remember what he'd said when I awoke and found myself alone. I reached out for Bernard, but only found his handkerchief from under his pillow, such a beautiful one, handrolled and very fine.

He came to collect us on Saturday evening and for once we were ready. Often there was a last-minute customer or a long telephone conversation or the garden would have to be watered—it was very dry that spring, cold but dry, and already the Green had brown patches. When we arrived at the Forbeses' house, there was Johnny waiting for us, sitting on the bear's back just as Marline used to do. His Dutch nurse was with him, smiling and remote, and there was no sign that there had been a great scene a few days previously. I hoped she could be persuaded to stay. I could hardly face Mrs. Vic again.

It started off being the usual sort of weekend. But after dinner we sat in the drawing-room and talked instead of playing records. It began as safe talk about the garden and what the gardener should plant and that sort of thing, but quite soon it turned to marriage. There we sat in our elegant armchairs, and talked about marriage.

The only obstacle Bernard could see was my having to give up the shop: "But I'll make it up to you, dearest. I'll give you shares in the gallery and you could be a director if you liked, a part-time one, of course. It would give you an interest and be a help to me. Strangely enough, Gertrude, who was always a tremendous help, refused to be a director. She said she wanted to be free with her help and not tied to it. She was rather like you in that respect."

I said, "It isn't only the shop, Bernard. It's love, or rather the lack of it. I'm deeply in love with you, but you hardly love me at all, which would put me at a terrible disadvantage, don't you agree?"

Bernard exclaimed rather indignantly, "Of course I love you. Perhaps I'm not 'in love,' but you know I love you." Then he left his formal chair and came close and put his arms round me and kissed me very tenderly. It was the first endearment he had given me in that house and I could feel myself being won over.

When I returned to Twickenham on Monday morning, we were engaged to be married in about two months' time. Bernard was quite calm about it and talked of a honeymoon in Madrid; but I felt strange and all shivery inside. It shouldn't be a difficult decision to make, marrying Bernard. It was a wonderful chance for a girl like me. Perhaps I was getting into a rut with my little shop and quiet life, and it wasn't much of a future for Tommy. I thought of her living in that beautiful house with Bernard as her stepfather and being able to have an expensive education, music—she was fond of music—and perhaps riding. There was little I could do for her on my own except to try and make her as happy as possible. I stood in my shop and looked round. The sun was shining through the pretty windows, but wasn't it rather dusty? Almost half the stock wasn't very attractive either—the Edwardian chamber-pot, for instance, the clumsy dining-table with insecure flaps, and the collection of not quite antique umbrella handles, what use were they to anybody? Of course there were some delightful things in the shop too, but were they worth becoming an old spinster for? I was nearly twenty-seven, with my face scarred and the mother of an illegitimate child. If I didn't make up my mind to marry soon, I never would.

I didn't tell Mary that I'd changed my mind about marrying Bernard because I knew she could so easily make me change my mind again. So I waited a few days until it was more established and I'd become used to the idea. Instead, I telephoned my mother, at least she'd be pleased.

As soon as she heard my voice, she snapped, "You're not in any trouble, are you?"

I said, "Well, not exactly trouble. I'm getting married and I thought you'd like to know."

There was a long pause: "Not to the child's father, that Brazilian or whatever he is?"

I laughed. "No, mother, it's someone you know."

Another pause. "It can't be Stephen; he's married to that dancing girl you encouraged him to marry. Good Heavens! It isn't Bernard, Bernard Forbes?"

I said, "Yes, mother, it's Bernard Forbes. We are getting married in about two months' time and planning to go to Madrid for our honeymoon." I was quite enjoying myself.

"But what about Tommy? Is he taking her on too?"

I snapped, "Of course, he's very fond of her. The two children will be brought up together as brother and sister. Oh, and mother, Bernard's offered me a directorship in his gallery."

I heard her calling, "Charlie, Charlie, come here!" and rang off. I guessed they'd be round in a day or two.

I went to Bernard's house one lunchtime to have a quiet talk with the staff. To my surprise Miss May almost gave notice on the spot when I told her Bernard and I were getting married. She said, "I suppose Mr. Forbes won't be needing me if you're living here permanently and not just at the weekends." I assured her we would still want to keep her on, but she appeared a little doubtful and muttered something about two mistresses in the house. On the other hand, dear old Mrs. Hicks was really pleased and so was Greta, and after a little persuading Greta agreed to stay for another six months: "Then Johnny will be old enough to go to a playschool in the mornings and you'll be able to manage the two children on your own," she suggested helpfully. I said I didn't quite know what I was doing except that I was giving up the shop. I was really glad that she had retracted her notice, otherwise we might have had to give up our Spanish honeymoon. It was only to be a short one, with business mixed with the honey, but if it was anything like our visit to Brussels it would be the happiest time in the world.

Every day I was becoming more accustomed to the idea of marrying Bernard. We didn't talk about it much together, our marriage, but when we did we both agreed to have a quiet registry office wedding. There was rather an attractive registry office in Richmond, with flowers, and almost as nice as a church. There was a garden too where hundreds of wedding groups had been photographed. I thought the air must have become impregnated with smiling brides as I watched two different groups arranging themselves self-consciously. I went there to inspect the place by myself and didn't mention it to Bernard.

When I told Mary that I was marrying Bernard after all she smiled and said she had already guessed. Although she didn't approve, she felt it was a thing I had to go through even if it crushed me, but added, "That fucking gallery won't be the same as our little shop." It was unlike her to use that word. We decided the best thing would be for Mary to let the shop because she hadn't the time to run it herself. Then she made a suggestion that really interested me. Why not store my favourite things in the basement of Bernard's house. It was only a semi-basement and not at all damp. Later on I might be able to arrange my things and have a room of my own down there, something very private. There was a large oak chest from Miss Murray's shop, which I could fill with my best china and other treasures, and there was a gilt console-table I was very fond of and the Trafalgar mirror that hung above it. One cannon ball of the mirror was missing and the glass was a little discoloured, but it was still very attractive. Carefully put away in my bedroom there were the twelve antique porcelain Meissen plates. They were too valuable to sell in our little shop, so I'd been keeping them on one side as an investment—they were from Miss Murray's collection. Our eyes darted round the shop. What about the Regency sofa, rather small, but so pretty, and the two mahogany dining-chairs with striped seats? "You must have something to sit on," Mary laughed. They belonged to Mary, but she insisted I have them and a Victorian tip-up table she had at home.

One minute we had been so happy making our arrangements and the next I found myself sitting on a queer little stool made from animals' horns—a most uncomfortable stool it was too—and crying my eyes out. I said, "Oh, Mary, suppose he won't let me put my things in his precious house. He may think I'm contaminating it or that Gertrude wouldn't like it. He is very strange that way." Then more brightly, "He might put up with the chest; there are several rather like it about the house. Anyway, I'll see what he says."

Mary said cynically, "If he won't let you put a few things in his basement before marriage, he never will afterwards."

On Sunday morning, when Bernard was entangled in a long telephone conversation, I went down to examine the basement. I had occasionally been down there before to speak to Peter, the picture restorer, but only into the room where he worked. There was a smaller room where he kept frames and work materials, quite a large hall with trunks stacked in one corner, and a long room that had a certain amount of sun and looked out on to the courtyard. It was empty except for some built-in cupboards, deed-boxes and a quantity of photographic material. There was more than enough room for the things I wanted to store and it had great possibilities for the future.

Later in the day, when we were having a pre-lunch drink, Bernard presented me with an engagement ring, a pinkish topaz surrounded by diamonds. It was a very unusual ring indeed and I was so touched and pleased to have it. It seemed almost too good for my work-worn hands, worn with the work I did in the shop. I am one of those women who like to use their bare hands when working, I feel all muffled up in protective gloves. Bernard didn't put the ring on my finger as men are supposed to do, he just gave me the little velvet case and said it was a small engagement present. He appeared quite embarrassed about it and there was no ceremony at all.

After I'd thanked him, and I thanked him very deeply, I asked if I could store some of my things in the front basement room. "It's only bits and pieces I don't want to part with," I said nervously. "The oak chest, for instance, it's so useful to store things in, and some Meissen plates that are rather valuable, twelve of them and not a single chip."

He looked thoughtful. "Well, I don't want a lot of junk here, tarnished gilt mirrors and things in glass cases and that kind of thing, but if you promise to keep it underground it can't do much harm. Not many things, mind."

To myself I said, "I'll put everything under sheets tightly packed in a corner," and to Bernard I said, "Oh, no, Bernard, there'll only be a couple of plain mahogany chairs and the things I pack in the chest. If I put them in the front room that Peter doesn't use they won't be in anyone's way." I slipped my arm round Bernard but, although he smiled, he didn't respond.

On Sundays we all had lunch together, the children, Greta and Miss May. Bernard sat at the head of the table with Johnny on one side and me on the other. He rather resented this family lunch but it gave him a chance to see more of Johnny and made for good relations with the staff. Miss May presided as if she were the hostess and I usually did something to help—laid the table, made sauces and quite often the pudding. Today I'd made the pudding, a lemon meringue pie, a favourite with the children. As I was taking it out of the fridge, Miss May suddenly noticed my ring and exclaimed, "Oh! Is that your engagement ring? Can I see it?" So I put down the slightly chilled pie and held out my left hand with pride. She examined the ring carefully and said: "It's secondhand, of course, but a lovely thing. You'll have to do something about your hands, though. They are not fit to wear a ring like that, are they?"

I looked into Miss May's face and saw that she disliked me very much and I thought to myself, "When my honeymoon is over I'll sack you."

25

It was very hot in Madrid, hotter than we expected in June. Then sometimes, in the shadow, a cold wind would come creeping round the corners. Our hotel had a large patio with a fountain playing in the middle of it and hotel guests sat at small tables in the shade under the arches. I'd never been to Spain before and thought of Spaniards as men with sombre dark faces under their black hats and perhaps with large moustaches sprouting from their upper lips; but I was years out of date—and there were no señoras disturbing the hot air with their fans either. The people we saw in the streets were little different to northerners except that they were darker and more formally dressed; but there was a delicious smell of coffee, vanilla and cigars, with a touch of brandy, coming from the bars where men sat talking to their friends. The women darted in and out of shops on their high heels or sauntered with their friends, all of them fashionably dressed and with so much care, and the middle-aged señoras, stout but still shapely, appeared to be almost proud of their excessive flesh, sailing over the pavements like swans.

We only had six clear days in Madrid and Bernard had a few business contacts to deal with, so we had to plan our time carefully. The main thing we wanted to see was the Prado. It quite overwhelmed us although Bernard knew what to expect. I managed a second visit while poor Bernard was discussing business with an important associate in a mixture of French, English and a smattering of Spanish. We had both learnt a little Spanish from Isabel and Catalina, but that didn't carry us far, and although Bernard had studied a lot during the last few weeks, it wasn't enough. I think not being able to speak Spanish properly put him out. He felt it undignified. Fortunately there was a Señor Castillo, who spoke perfect English and enjoyed using it. He was a charming man with a subtle sense of humour, and generous and kind too. He drove us to Toledo in his imported English car and we spent a few hours there, but I could have stayed for weeks in that ancient and proud city perched on its hill and almost surrounded by the river Tagus. The architecture was so impressive we almost forgot to look at El Greco's paintings.

On Sunday I very much wanted to visit the Rastro, the famous flea market our friend had told us about. He said you could buy anything there—carved angels, barrel organs, crystal chandeliers, antique dolls, furniture, all the kind of things I loved; but when I mentioned it to Bernard, as we were eating our breakfast in bed, he was very against it. "What, spend this beautiful day with the fleas! Certainly not. We'll go to the Retiro, we've hardly seen it at all. I know, we'll hire a boat and I'll row you on the river or lake, I'm not sure which it is, but you'll love it. It will be far better than having our wallets stolen by the fleas."

So we went to the Retiro, a lovely park, larger than Hyde Park, I think. At first we enjoyed walking among the people, but later we walked almost alone under the trees and then in a rose garden. Eventually we came to a bar beside the water and sat there drinking cool beer and watching the people in the boats. It was very like a Renoir painting and, when Bernard rowed our hired boat, it was as if we were part of the painting too. I'd never seen Bernard so lighthearted as he was that day. We were like a typical newly-married couple, we kissed under the trees and there wasn't a sign of Gertrude anywhere.

We were to leave Madrid at lunchtime on the Monday. But before we left we paid a quick visit to the Escorial. Señor Castillo called for us early in the morning, saying we couldn't leave Madrid without seeing it. We were afraid that the visit would result in us arriving late at the airport, but it was worth the little worry, although we didn't enter the building except for a few minutes in the church. We walked round the gardens and saw the building from different angles, such a beautiful place built with great simplicity, Doric I think it is called.

It must have been standing there for nearly four hundred years but was in a wonderful state of preservation, and so immense and severe, but glowed tenderly in the shafts of early-morning sunlight.

It was so early we were practically the only people there and we wandered freely. The air was cool and very pure and made us feel hungry so we drove the little way to a pretty village nestling against the mountains and had breakfast of coffee, rolls and peaches. I thought it would be an attractive place to live in, but Señor Castillo said that although it was a popular resort for Madrileños during the summer, it was bitterly cold in winter. As we drove away I looked back and had a strange feeling that I would come back one day and that I would be alone when I came. I suppose most of us get these feelings and they sometimes come true, but I didn't like to think I'd be alone when next I came.

Señor Castillo (we called him Eduardo now we were friends) drove us to the hotel to collect our luggage and then to the airport, and presented me with a large bouquet of mixed flowers when we parted. It must have been hidden in the boot of the car and he was pleased to see my surprise. There were cigars for Bernard too, but we had nothing for him; so we asked him to stay with us in Richmond and he seemed to like the idea.

We arrived home to find the children having tea with Greta in the garden and each of us grabbed our own child to hold close and to kiss their honey-smeared faces. There were presents to be given and news to hear and for Bernard a great pile of letters, which he took into his study. Later on I went upstairs and, from force of habit, opened the door of the room I'd always shared with Tommy. There were piles of suitcases containing my clothes that Mary had brought round, and my dresses and coats were hanging in the wardrobe, and someone had laid out my nightgown and put my rather downtrodden slippers under the bed. I felt too tired to face the unpacking that evening and the light would disturb Marline. I'd only take what I needed for the night into Bernard's room.

I picked out a few things and crossed the landing and entered the large room. Bernard's suitcase was already opened and clothes were scattered over the bed. A cramping sadness settled on me as I slowly moved towards the great wardrobe and opened the door and saw what I knew I'd see—Gertrude's clothes, hanging in an almost menacing way as if they were made of concrete. I opened the drawers and there were her hand-embroidered underclothes, exquisite things that had never been near a chain store. They would have fitted Charlotte, why hadn't she taken them away? There was the newly-cleaned blue dressing-gown, hanging possessively from its peg. Timidly, I felt in the pockets and found a neatly-folded clean handkerchief in one and a tortoise-shell comb inlaid with silver in the other. Feeling I was prying I took my hands away from the soft blue material and wiped them on my skirt, then slowly went downstairs to Bernard's study.

He was not allowed to be disturbed there, but I went in and disturbed him. He was sitting at his desk with the gold pen I'd given him as a wedding present in his beautiful hand. I was as proud of his hands as if they had been my own. "Oh, Bernard!" I said reproachfully, "where am I to sleep? Gertrude's things are all over the room and there's nowhere to put anything. Why didn't you give them to Charlotte or some charity? Do you realize they've been there for nearly three years?"

He looked at me as if I were despicable: "Are you suggesting I give my wife's clothes to some charity, the Salvation Army perhaps?"

I said bravely, "Well, that's up to you, or they could be sold and the money given to her favourite charity. Do you remember? She liked the Greenpeace people."

Dropping the gold pen as if it were burning his hand, he said, "I know what my wife likes and dislikes and she certainly does not want all and sundry wearing her clothes. Go away now, we'll talk about this problem tomorrow in a rational way. You are very aggressive, Bella. Overtired, I suppose."

Dismissed, I left the room and saw Miss May's straight back glide towards the kitchen, and as I went upstairs she called, "Good night." I went to the bedroom that I'd shared with Marline for almost four years. She was asleep in her little bed by the wall; sometimes it was moved to Johnny's room but usually she slept with me. I'd left my night things on Bernard's bed—or should I say "Bernard and Gertrude's bed"? I couldn't bring myself to visit that morbid room again that evening, so I took a fresh nightgown from a suitcase that I'd packed so hopefully a week ago, undressed and crept into bed. I felt homesick for my small room over the shop.

During the night I saw Bernard standing by my bed and I was almost frightened of him, he looked so tall standing there in the moonlight. He bent and kissed me on the forehead as a parent would and said, "I'm sorry, Bella, we will discuss the problem of the clothes tomorrow, the sleeping arrangements too. We'll sort it out, my dear," then he draped something over a chair, saying, "You left this on my bed," and went away. It was my nightgown.

We met at breakfast as if nothing had happened and Miss May fluttered round us to make sure we had everything we wanted. "Have you all you want, dear?" she asked me in a mocking way and I assured her that I had. I could hear Marline's voice in the kitchen and jumped up from the table nervously and said I must get her ready for her school in Twickenham; but Bernard said he couldn't take her that morning because something important was to be delivered to the house. "She's already missed a week, so another day won't hurt her," he added in relaxed tones and continued to munch his brown toast until there was a ring at the front door bell and Mrs. Hicks came to tell us that someone was asking for me, he wouldn't come in.

I went to the door followed by Bernard. He had an amused smile on his face and last night's troubles seemed to have vanished. Standing by the bear there was a man who looked like a mechanic and he asked if I was Mrs. Forbes (I think it was the first time anyone had called me that). Then he said he'd come to deliver the car and Bernard and I followed him to the gate and there in the street was a little lemon-coloured Fiat, Bernard's wedding present to me. The man handed me the keys and some papers and went away and the car was mine. I hadn't driven since the accident—although I hadn't been driving myself at the time—but this little car looked so friendly and harmless I thought we'd get on very well together if I had a little practice. Then Bernard told me to look through the papers, and there was a receipt for six driving lessons, a refresher course, he said. With Marline in the back we went for a short drive round the park, Bernard driving because I had no licence or insurance. I hadn't wished for a car since the accident but now I owned this dear little Fiat, I was more than pleased. I couldn't thank Bernard enough.

When the evening came, we sat rather self-consciously in the drawing-room, with Gertrude's clothes like a heavy cloud between us. We couldn't bring ourselves to talk about them, so we talked about the gallery instead. Bernard thought I should work there twice a week and see how I liked it. One day in the office and one in the gallery. There was a Miss Rose, a Jewess, who would be a great help, he said, and added kindly, "You may become as devoted to the gallery as you were to your shop."

Quite shocked I exclaimed that would be impossible, it wouldn't be mine.

"No, it would be ours," he said coldly and I could see he was hurt.

"Yes, of course," I said quickly, "I'd quite forgotten that. I was looking on it as a kind of job, not something we were involved in together." Suddenly I couldn't bear it any longer and I rushed to Bernard and buried my face in his shoulder, although I knew he didn't like being touched unexpectedly. "Dear Bernard," I cried, "what are we to do about poor Gertrude's clothes and things? We can't let them ruin our life together."

26

IN THE end we reached a compromise, not a perfect one, but quite a sensible arrangement, in which we both had to give way a little and adjust ourselves. Bernard agreed to have all Gertrude's things packed away in trunks, with lists of their contents attached instead of labels, and three new trunks arrived accompanied by Miss Rose from the gallery and it was she who was to do the packing. She had been working for Bernard for a good many years and he trusted her; also she was exactly the right person for the job, reliable and impersonal. I had met her once or twice in Bernard's office, but this was the first time we had really talked to each other and I liked and respected her. Later on she was a great help to me when I was working at the Forbes Gallery. If she thought Bernard's obsession for his dead wife strange, she never said so. She didn't pry and revel in it like Miss May.

It was obvious that Bernard didn't want to share his matrimonial bed with me. He felt in some way that he was being disloyal to Gertrude and found it almost impossible to make love to me in the house they had shared together with so much happiness. In that house I wasn't his wife, I was the little protégée and in time it became a great strain being the little protégée day and night. Besides almost worshipping Bernard I had this very strong physical love for him; just to put my hand against his face so overwhelmed me that tears came to my eyes.

The large carved bed that Bernard and Gertrude had slept in all their married life, the bed in which Gertrude had died, was dismantled and taken down to the basement, fortunately not to the room where the things from the shop were stored. Two modern beds with elaborate headboards were installed. I don't know who chose them—they were very un-Forbes—but they were wonderfully comfortable. The hardly-mentioned agreement between us was that Bernard was free to sleep in his dressing-room without reproach. Occasionally he asked me to join him there, but it was never a success from a loving point of view because of his obsession with Gertrude— it was almost as if she were in the room. I suggested moving from the house, but he said he couldn't part with it and he wanted Johnny to grow up in the house of his mother. It was as if he thought she had impregnated the walls and could influence her child.

It was a pity that we had so much difficulty discussing our problems, particularly Bernard, who was a very private man and hated to admit that anything was wrong. But once we had faced our difficulties and adjusted to them, life together was much easier and sometimes almost happy. We enjoyed our children, entertained a little and were entertained in return, and I was fairly interested in the gallery although my work consisted of writing business letters in French. Miss Rose coached me in this or sat at a desk in the main room near the entrance, handing out catalogues and that sort of thing. Bernard's elegant young assistant did most of the talking. He became quite animated when he discussed paintings, otherwise he was a little unhuman.

The gallery was pretty quiet just then, only mixed exhibitions; but Miss Rose said that when the summer was over there would be one-man exhibitions with private views that were like cocktail parties, attended by critics and famous people. She did her best to arouse my interest and I *was* interested in the paintings, but the gallery seemed a little dull after my cheerful little shop. For one thing, the actual buying and selling was so discreet. Besides this, although it was summer I had to wear stuffy tights and formal shoes; no jeans, of course, nothing comfortable, so I wore a silver-grey dress with a narrow skirt that was difficult to sit down in. Still, I only went to the gallery two or three times a week and I was pleased that Bernard wanted me there, particularly when he introduced me to his business friends as his wife. I was so proud to have such a husband. The days I stayed at home seemed to pass very quickly. Although Greta looked after the children most of the time, she had days off and I helped her, particularly now Marline was home with her school closed for the holidays. I sometimes took them out for the day in my small car, once to the sea, where Johnny's white skin suffered from the sun. Bernard was very angry about this and said that I was only used to looking after piccaninnies and wasn't to be trusted with fine-skinned white children. It was very unlike him to say such a thing and the next day, when the redness had faded, he was very contrite and, of course, I forgave him. All the same, this thing he had said in his anger stayed in my mind like a thorn although I tried to forget it.

The car made such a difference to my life. I didn't use it to go to the gallery because I went in Bernard's and I wasn't up to driving in the centre of London yet; but it was so useful for shopping, visiting my few friends and taking Marline to school in term time. Best of all, it gave me a new confidence. I suppose I felt rather as my mother did in her red Rover.

I didn't see much of my mother at this time because Mr. Crimony was ill, really ill, poor man, and waiting to go into hospital for an operation; but she had come to our simple registry office wedding—nothing would have kept her away from that—and I heard her say to Mr. Crimony in her usual abrupt way: "You silly old man, you would choose a time like this to be ill." All dressed in black, he sat outside in the car and neither of them came to the wedding lunch, which we had in a local French restaurant. So beside ourselves, there were just the two witnesses, business friends of Bernard's, Mary and Peter. Peter was particularly quiet that day. Mary was very gay at first, but by the end of the meal tears were pouring down her small pointed face. She said champagne always made her weep, and when we left for our plane, she was laughing again.

Poor Mr. Crimony. Mother did bring him to see the house once before he returned to the hospital for his second operation. Marline was delighted to see her Mr. Chimney again and showed him round the garden and allowed him to watch her feeding the magpies, which she had been taming all the summer. When the cock bird settled on her shoulder and took food from between her lips, the old man thought it dangerous, and I must admit, I did at first. But the birds appeared to be absolutely trustworthy except that they were thieves. When the last young magpie left the nest—there had only been two—I intended to have a good search for Bernard's golden cuff-link. I was sure it was somewhere in that domed nest.

My mother showed Mr. Crimony all over the house and, although it took some time and he appeared to be very tired, I think he enjoyed it and liked to think of such a fine place "being in the family," as he called it. He saw little Johnny in his nursery and thought him a nice little chap "but not a patch on our Tommy."

When we were sitting at the dining-room table, mother picked up a heavy silver tablespoon and weighed it in her hand as if to tell its worth and said, "I must say, you've done very well for yourself, Bella. I never would have thought it possible."

But Mr. Crimony said: "It's no surprise to me. Bella always knew what she wanted. If she'd stayed in my coal office, where would she be now?"

I laughed and said, "In the coal office, I should imagine."

Just a week later Mr. Crimony died during his second operation.

27

ON THE first day of the new term I took Marline to school. Then I returned to do something I could only do when she was not at home—search for Bernard's cuff-link in the magpies' nest. I carried a small ladder and a child's spade down to the juniper tree clearing. I was relieved to see there wasn't a single magpie in sight, and I put the ladder against the cherry tree and climbed up. I found the spade, small as it was, useless; something flexible was needed, a hand for instance, so I dropped the spade and put my hand in through the opening of the dome-shaped nest and scooped up all kinds of filth—bird mess, dirty feathers and a few small bones, a child's bead necklace, sweet papers, but then the golden cuff-link. I had not damaged the nest at all, just given it a good clean, but suddenly an angry bird appeared and began to attack me, making frightful noises at the same time. I managed to beat it off my face but got my hand scratched by its strong dark beak and by the time I'd reached the bottom of the ladder there were two of them attacking me. I could still hear their harsh, aggressive cries as I ran towards the house.

Later in the day, when I went to retrieve the ladder, the cock bird appeared threateningly and from that time Gertrude's *elsters* never trusted me again. Bernard was pleased to have his cuff-link back, though.

Johnny was nearly three and rather spoilt by Bernard and Marline; I suppose we all spoilt him in a way because Bernard insisted that he must always have his own way. If he wanted to eat from the back of his plate he must be allowed to do so. When he cried at bedtime, he could stay up as long as he wanted, often falling asleep on the carpet.

It could have been much worse except that by nature he was an obedient boy, particularly when his father was not around. I suggested to Bernard that he went to playschool in the mornings, as there was one for under fives quite near. Reluctantly he agreed and for the first few days Johnny enjoyed himself. He was very affectionate towards the other children and not at all shy as I feared he would be. Then one morning he was tired from staying up too late the previous evening and, when he saw Bernard, he broke into tears and said he didn't want to go to school. Bernard held him in his arms and said, "Poor little fellow, of course you needn't go to school if you don't like it. We'll try again when you are older." And that was the end of school for the time being.

We had done nothing about the replacement of Greta, who was due to leave in late October. I offered her a rise in salary if she would stay a little longer, until Christmas, perhaps, but she was determined to go home. It was Miss May I wanted to get rid of, not Greta, who had become quite a friend. We hardly needed her as well as old Mrs. Hicks. She was over-inquisitive and too interested in our sleeping arrangements and because of this I used to change the sheets so that it appeared that Bernard slept in the bed beside me and not in the dressing-room. I only did this on Mondays, when she put clean linen on the beds after I left the house. One Monday, just as I was leaving and Bernard was sitting in the car waiting for me, Miss May caught my arm familiarly and said, "I hope you haven't been juggling about with the sheets, Mrs. Forbes. It's quite unnecessary. I know your husband sleeps in his dressing-room."

I jerked my arm free but didn't say a thing, just walked away with what must have been a stricken face. I could hear Bernard saying, "Hurry, dear, we're late," then seeing my face as he opened the car door for me, he asked, "What's happened? You are upset about something," and he put his arm round me in the kindest way.

I told him what Miss May had said and asked if he'd mind if I got rid of her, she was so very unpleasant at times. He agreed that it was time she went and offered to dismiss her that evening, but I said I'd prefer to do it myself. I did it so well that she left the following morning and nothing was said about a month's notice on either side.

It was the dismissal of Miss May that caused me to give up my career in the gallery. It was intended as a temporary break until we got someone suitable to help at home; but it gradually became permanent. I did go to some of the private views and helped out occasionally when Miss Rose was short-handed, but that was all.

At the end of October, just before Greta returned to Holland, we picked apples in the spinney. There was a small tree of indeterminate cookers and a large one of Blenheim orange, apples as beautiful as their name in appearance and taste. To my surprise Peter left his magnifying glass and paints and joined us. He climbed the trees with a basket on his arm, but Greta and I used a ladder. Marline had been given a holiday that day and was climbing about like a monkey. Johnny, who was only just three, had to be carefully carried up and down every now and then to pick a few apples, but otherwise he sat on the grass or collected windfalls from the ground. It was a perfect autumn day and we made an occasion of the apple gathering or rather picking, by having a picnic under the tree.

In all the time I'd been connected with the Forbeses and since becoming a Forbes myself, I'd seldom seen Peter outside the rooms where he worked, a largish studio upstairs where he did his painting and restoring and a room in the basement he used for picture framing and other things. He often worked with a small magnifying-glass fixed in one eye like a monocle and I almost thought of it as part of his pale calm face. When the apple picking was over he helped me store the apples in the room where my things were kept. I took off the shroud-like sheets and showed him my treasures and from that moment we were close friends.

He cared for antiques almost as much as I did. In his spare time he decorated the room for me, all white except for a sea-green ceiling, which rather gave the feeling of being in an aquarium. We covered the rough wood floor with a light terracotta fitted carpet, my only extravagance at that time. Then Peter discovered a beautiful fireplace that had been boarded in and the room completely lost its basement look. When the furniture was arranged it was transformed into a magical place. Bernard knew nothing about it and he sometimes wondered why Johnny, who liked to play there and called it "Bella's house" tried to lead him down the basement steps. If he had looked through the basement windows, he would have seen Bella's house in all its glory and his special chair waiting for him; but Bernard wasn't the kind of man who looked down into basements and I wasn't sure if I wanted him to or not. I'd have loved to have seen him in his chair and to be sitting at his feet as I used to, perhaps with him stroking my hair; but we never sat like that now. Would it be different in Bella's house? I felt I'd rather not know.

Soon after Greta left I engaged a daily nurse, a policeman's wife who had been a nanny before she married, Jenny she was called. Her hours were flexible and she was willing to stay late when we went out in the evening, which was once a week at the most. On other evenings we sometimes had people to dinner, otherwise we listened to music, read or looked at television. We didn't talk as much as we used to, and I think it was about this time that Bernard lost interest in educating me. All the same, he was a kind and generous husband and he did want me to be happy. It put him out if I wasn't, so quite often I appeared to be happier than I was. Sometimes I had hopes that Gertrude was fading from the house because he had ceased to talk about her as if she were still alive.

One autumn morning I drove to the Green and the leaves were falling from the chestnut trees and I remembered how I watched them from the shop window and used to think of them as golden gloves falling down. Now I was the other side of the window looking in and instead of antiques there were tubes of paint and drawing blocks and stark white canvases, brushes too and art books. Mary had told me that it was now an art shop, but I hadn't really taken it in and now, seeing the changes, I felt slightly shocked and resentful. I could see the owner of the shop, a man with a pink drooping face and pig-like nose, wrapping up a neat square parcel, then putting money in the till. I'd never had a till, only a black tin cashbox. Suddenly my resentment faded and I hoped little Droopy-cheeks would make a great success of his shop, far better to sell art materials. The shop was now completely impersonal and nothing to do with me. That part of my life was finished. But I still had my collection in Bella's house and was adding to it from time to time.

After Christmas Marline went to a new school, rather an expensive one where the children wore a very pretty casual uniform. She stayed there all day and seemed to like it, making friends and bringing them home to tea. There were birthday parties and I always seemed to be buying birthday presents for children I'd never even seen; but I had my small income from the building society and there was nothing much to spend it on except Marline and my collection downstairs. Mr. Crimony had left Marline and me a thousand pounds each, which I immediately put in our accounts. The rest of his money went to my mother, so she was quite a well off woman now and gave up her travel agency work. This was a mistake because she found life without Mr. Crimony to boss around very lonely and I think she bossed people in the agency and must have missed that too. She took to visiting me at least once a week, usually for tea, when Marline was home from school. She got on extraordinarily well with Marline, and now she had overcome her original shock at her colour, I don't think she would have changed her for a white grand-daughter. She was fond of Johnny too and used to tell people that she was his grandmother if she got the chance.

Seeing her pleasure in her grand-children, I asked her why she had so disliked me as a child. She said quite truthfully that it was because I reminded her of my father and that I'd brought her shame. "You see," she said sadly, "it was what they call a shotgun wedding. The whole thing was so humiliating. Producing a baby six months after marriage was a terrible thing in those days, so of course I resented you and I resented your father also because he didn't love me, but was fond of you. I knew he'd go off with someone in the end and that's what he did. I felt so bitter towards you both. I suppose in my way I loved the wretched man and that made it worse. You are very lucky, Bella, to have such a devoted husband, very lucky indeed." Mother was someone else I had to wear a happy face for.

I was fairly busy at this time. Now Miss May had gone away I did all the cooking and some of the housework. Mrs. Hicks did all the heavy work—and there was a lot in that large house—and she also insisted on preparing the vegetables because she had always done so when Gertrude was alive. Jenny fitted in extremely well, arriving soon after eight in the morning to help the children dress and to supervise their breakfast which they ate in the kitchen. Bernard and I ate a stately breakfast in the dining-room, discussing our correspondence of which I had very little, and the gallery which he liked to talk about with me. Then he made a few suggestions on how I was to spend the day, gave me a peck on the cheek and would go off in search of Peter to discuss his work. Peter always worked in the house, never in the gallery.

On weekdays there wasn't much cooking until the evening so I often had a morning more or less free to visit art exhibitions suggested by Bernard and then go off to the sale rooms. I became quite bold at the sales and sometimes bid for things that ran into hundreds of pounds, at least a few hundred pounds. I bought a French escritoire made of beautifully inlaid woods for £230 and sold my early Victorian one for £65 in the following week's sale to pay for some of it. A pair of elegant Queen Anne pier glasses took the place of the Trafalgar mirror, one on either side of the console table; then the console table was changed for an earlier, more elaborately carved one, and so it went on and the contents of my secret room became more and more valuable. I wouldn't have been able to do it without Peter's help and the use of his van, and it was he who found some of my best bargains. We'd sit down there drinking coffee and planning what to do next and sometimes Mary joined us. She called the room "Paradise Lost," but I thought it was more "Paradise Found."

28

JOHNNY started having nightmares, so Bernard had his small bed moved to the dressing-room and he slept beside his father and the nightmares ceased. I was glad for the child's sake, and yet I could not help feeling a certain resentment. Now, when the children played together and Johnny cried because he couldn't have his own way, Bernard would appear from nowhere and accuse Marline of being rough with him. If they were telling him something both at once, as they so often did, he'd say, "Marline, be quiet for a moment and let Johnny speak." Sometimes she seemed a little hurt, but on the whole she took it very well. When I looked at my daughter I loved her so much, and when I looked at my stepson, with his fairy-story red and white cheeks, it cut me to the heart and I'd think: "He'll always come first with his father. Marline and I are nothing." I became almost jealous of the child, and I'm sorry to say I sometimes gave him a slap when he was particularly difficult. He wasn't naturally a difficult child; Bernard had made him so.

We picked the apples again a few days before Johnny's fourth birthday. It wasn't the happy day it had been the previous year, perhaps because I tried too hard. We had our picnic under the tree and Mary was there as well as Peter, so it should have been a jolly occasion, and it was for the children. Johnny was far more nimble this year and climbed about the lower branches of the tree although we were terrified he'd fall. Bernard would never forgive us if a big black bruise appeared on his snow-white skin. He didn't fall, but anything made me nervous that afternoon. One minute I'd be laughing, then I'd find I was crying instead and Peter and Mary would exchange glances.

I knew they were worried about me and indeed I was worried about myself. As my desolate marriage deteriorated, so did my health. I had headaches and found it difficult to eat, the food seemed to stick in my throat; but the worst thing was the depression, sometimes really black and terrible, and at other times just under the surface waiting to pounce. I'd sit in my secret room and tears would run down my cheeks; then, when I touched the beautiful things—the carving on the console table, the smooth inlaid woods of the escritoire and the Spanish virgin with her delicately carved hands and gold-embroidered robes—I'd feel comforted and I'd return to the household upstairs. There was only Mrs. Hicks working for us now both children went to school, Johnny just in the morning. The policeman's wife still came to babysit, but it wouldn't be for long because she was expecting a baby of her own. We went out so seldom now, Bernard and I, that that wouldn't cause much inconvenience.

Meanwhile a girl called Alison had come into our lives, a wistful girl with small breasts and large eyes that appeared to be appealing for help. She worked in Bernard's bank and had cashed cheques for him for over a year without him noticing her. Then she turned up at the gallery one lunchtime and he recognized her immediately, quite startled to see her against a different background. He told me about her when we were having dinner one evening. "There was this timid girl gazing at the paintings with her big eyes and trying to understand them. She said she often spent her lunch hour in the National Gallery but now she was becoming interested in modern paintings after a visit to the Tate. The poor girl—she's called Alison, by the way—admitted she knew nothing about art, but she so wanted to learn. Anyway, I promised to lend her some books and she'll be calling for them on Saturday afternoon. You won't mind giving her tea, will you?"

No, I wouldn't mind giving her tea. And that's how Alison crept into our lives. I do so hope poor Gertrude didn't look on me as a kind of Alison. I think, I'm almost sure, she accompanied Bernard on some of his trips to Brussels and she didn't have to study French first.

And now comes a terrible time, a time when I behaved quite out of character. It was as if my brain had turned into broken elastic. It had been so stretched and strained in one way or another and it was as if I had lost the control of it. The disaster occurred the day after the apple picking. It had been quite a pleasant day, really, and with Johnny's help I was storing the apples in the basement hall. There was a long shelf near the gas meters that took about thirty pounds of apples and I decided to put the rest in my big chest, which had been banished from my room because of its clumsy farmhouse appearance. It had a great heavy lid and a great heavy iron lock and it now stood in a dark corner of the hall. It was difficult to open at first and I pulled it a little way from the wall to make it easier. It was empty except for a slight smell of camphor, so I left it open to air for a little.

While the chest was airing Peter came down the stairs carrying a suitcase. He said he was going to stay in Cornwall with his family for a few days and had come to say goodbye. Johnny wanted to see him drive off in his little red mail van, so we trooped up the basement steps into the sunny courtyard and Johnny climbed on to the bear's back as most young children always did. People passing the gate must have thought what a happy-looking family we were with our beautiful, laughing child and stately house, though they might have wondered at Peter's funny little van.

When he had driven away we went down the steps with great care because Bernard said they were dangerous, but when we reached the bottom step Johnny pulled away and started picking up the brilliant apples and roughly flinging them into the chest, laughing defiantly when I told him to stop. Then he started to climb into the chest.

I shouted, "No!" and ran across the room and made to grab him, but before I reached him the lid came down, the lid came down, THE LID CAME DOWN. There was nobody to be seen, just the heavy closed lid. For the rest of my life I'd have to live with that great black lid coming crashing down.

Could I have been quicker, calmer? Could I have saved the child? Was I to blame for leaving the chest open? Before I opened it I thought I knew what I'd find—a little dead boy with a defiant laugh on his face. But when I saw him, his mouth was pulled down as if in horror and his eyes had gone all startled in a dreadful way. As I held my poor stepboy in my arms I lost my reason and it was as if I had become someone else, someone stupid and crafty at the same time. At all costs Bernard must never know what had happened to his son. I must find somewhere to hide him. It never occurred to my poor twisted mind to telephone for help; an ambulance could have been there in a matter of minutes. I laid him down on the dirty floor and ran upstairs to fetch one of Bernard's fine handkerchiefs to wind round his neck to support his head. This seemed very important to me, rather like sticking a doll's broken head together. But it didn't work. His head still lolled. Then I remembered the kiss of life and kissed and kissed him; but it made no difference because he was certainly quite dead. All the same, I wrapped my cardigan round him because he appeared to be already growing cool.

My main idea was to hide him from Bernard. I would bury him in the garden. So I put him back in the chest while I went out to dig. The obvious place was under the juniper tree where his mother used to sit and dream before he was born. The earth was very soft and leafy there and it was easy to dig a shallow grave. I collected some strawberry plants which grew wild in that part of the garden and put them beside the grave to plant over it later on. Then I heard the church clock strike the half hour and realized it was almost time Marline returned from school, so I ran back to the house to close the lid of the chest, which I'd left open in the wild hope that he might come alive again, that a miracle might have occurred and he'd just be sleeping. I felt his forehead, but it was definitely growing colder and his little hands didn't feel like Johnny's. His arms had gone strangely heavy and fell back when I lifted them. All the same, there would still have been time to call for help but I couldn't face Bernard and reveal what had happened and my poor twisted mind could only think of that. I remembered with relief that he would be late home that evening. He was taking Alison to a concert; she had now become interested in music as well as art.

I didn't go near the basement again until Marline was safely in bed. I usually read the children a story at bedtime. They took turns in choosing it and this evening it was Johnny's turn and Marline kept asking where he was. I told her Charlotte and her husband had taken Johnny away for a few days motoring holiday. Later on I told Bernard the same lie, polished up a little, and he believed me because he didn't see my eyes flicker as they do when I tell lies. But he was very annoyed with Charlotte for taking his son away without his permission. He grumbled, "I don't like it at all. He didn't even say goodbye to me."

And I turned my face away and said, "He wanted to go, you know how he is," and we parted for the night, Bernard to his room with the little boy's empty bed beside his.

When I saw that Marline was asleep, I went downstairs and took Johnny out of the chest and wrapped him in my best silk dress, the colour of maize. I felt nothing was good enough for him. He was cold now and his face looked beautiful, even more beautiful than in life; but he was unexpectedly heavy to carry through the garden and into the spinney.

I found I was talking to him as if he were alive: "What a heavy boy you are, Johnny! We'll soon be there now," and as I put him in the little grave, "Oh, my darling little boy! I don't know what's going to happen now." As I covered him with the leafy earth there was a faint rustle and I felt I was being observed; but it was only the magpies, their white feathers showing in the bright moonlight. There appeared to be more than usual, but they were quite quiet, only watching.

I planted the strawberry plants as well as I could, but didn't like to water them because of Johnny getting wet. Then I sat on Gertrude's bench and remembered how she had asked me to look after her child if anything happened to her. Well, I had looked after him to the best of my ability except for an occasional slap. It was Bernard who had spoilt him. I stayed on the bench for a long time thinking, and I kept shivering although it was a warm night.

29

I DON'T know how I would have got through the next two days if I hadn't found a discarded bottle of Valium in Miss May's room, the extra strong blue ones. They must have been there for years but they were still potent. There were sleeping pills too. They numbed my poor brain in a marvellous way, and although I was more or less in a dream, I managed to do the cooking without any disasters. Bernard said, "You are not yourself, Bella. Are you ill?" I told him another lie. I said I had a touch of flu.

He stayed at home on Johnny's birthday, his fourth it would have been. He was convinced that Charlotte would bring him home on such an important day and insisted that I prepared a large family lunch and all the things that Johnny liked, stuffed chicken and roast potatoes and a chocolate pudding with whipped cream. I said there wasn't time for a birthday cake so he went out and bought one. As I worked in the kitchen tears ran down my cheeks; but I had had these crying fits for some time so Mrs. Hicks wasn't surprised. Bernard returned with the cake and said it was a beautiful day outside and wouldn't I leave the kitchen for a little walk round the garden with him, it would do my cold good. So we walked among the last of the autumn flowers still brilliant and untouched by frost. Bernard was holding my arm, and we were closer together than we had been for months. I thought, "This is the last time we shall walk together in a loving way. When Johnny's grave is discovered, it will be the end of everything between us. Perhaps Bernard will think of me with horror." I had a sudden idea and told Bernard I must leave him, there was an important letter I must write immediately. And I took his hand away from my arm and held it against my face for a moment, then ran into the house.

Mrs. Hicks was in the dining-room laying the table for the expected family lunch and I thought if only it were true and Johnny would come running into the room followed by Charlotte and the husband we'd never seen. I asked Mrs. Hicks to keep an eye on the oven for me and she said she would, but added, "I only hope Mr. Forbes won't be disappointed. Strange them not sending a card or telephoning. Perhaps Miss Charlotte has forgotten the date of the poor child's birthday."

I said, "Perhaps," and opened the drinks cupboard and selected a bottle of brandy and went upstairs with it.

I settled down to write my letter in Marline's room; it was more private than my bedroom. I fetched a tooth mug and the little bottle of Valium from the bathroom and counted the tablets. There were only ten left, but there was plenty of alcohol to help them down; a tumbler of brandy would be almost lethal on its own—I wondered if I was allowed to mix water with it. I took a sip of the neat brandy, then wrote my letter on a large sheet of Marline's drawing paper I found pinned to a board. There was the beginning of a drawing in the top left-hand corner, a happy drawing of flowers and leaves and not very suitable for the letter I was about to write. I addressed it to Bernard and anyone else who should read it, a coroner perhaps. I didn't want the letter to be too personal, just very truthful.

I gave a detailed account of exactly what happened from the time I opened the chest to air it and Johnny said goodbye to Peter: the careful journey down the steps, Johnny wildly throwing the apples into the open chest, me telling him to stop it, and how in defiance he climbed into it although I shouted "No" (actually, I couldn't quite remember if he was standing upright or rather bent forward, I thought it was bent forward) and so on. I wrote very quickly because it was agony to recall what happened. It was difficult to explain why I was so afraid of Bernard that I had to bury the poor little body under the juniper tree. I appealed to Bernard to forgive me for acting in such a strange manner and asked if he had noticed my depression and mental deterioration during the last few months. I felt I was losing my sanity and, now I was the indirect cause of his son's death, I couldn't go on any longer. I did point out that if Johnny had not been encouraged to be disobedient, his death might not have occurred. I said little about love or the pain of parting because it would be read by strangers. I felt calmer after I'd written the letter and I put it on my bedside table with the brandy and Valium. I planned to lie down after lunch and tell Bernard to call me when Charlotte came, which would be a long, long time.

I closed my bedroom door and ran downstairs to help Mrs. Hicks with the meal for people who would never arrive and put candles on a birthday cake for a boy who was already dead. At one o'clock Marline came home from school because she had remembered it was Johnny's birthday. She had bought him red slippers decorated with fluffy rabbits' heads with flopping ears. She was rather tearful when we eventually sat down to eat our lunch at the half-empty table; but Bernard tried to appear more cheerful than he was, complimenting me on the cooking and suggesting how easy it would be to heat up when the rest of the family arrived. He said that it was such a perfect autumn day and that he was feeling quite lighthearted. "Cheer up, little Marlinchen," he said, giving her hair a playful tweak, "Johnny will be home this evening." Then turning to me, he said, "And why aren't you eating, Bella, dear?"

I told him I felt uneasy, as if a heavy storm were coming: "It must be the flu. I'll lie down this afternoon and have a really long rest, so don't disturb me until Charlotte comes."

Before we had finished our late meal, there was a ring at the front door bell and we could hear Mrs. Hicks talking to some men in the hall. Bernard left the table and I could hear his authoritative voice. "Yes, it could well be true. We have a nest down in the thicket. Been there for some years ... cuff-links ... no objection at all ..."

Marline, alert as always, bounded from the room crying, "My birds! You mustn't frighten them or they'll go away."

Then Bernard, reprovingly: "Be quiet, Marline, go back to the dining-room and finish your meal."

Marline did not return, but at least she was quiet, and when they walked through the drawing-room into the garden she was trotting behind. I stood there holding on to the door, watching them. I was weighed down by fear and felt so ill and anxious my teeth chattered— yet it was as if I had fire in my veins—but I had to follow the little troop of three men and a child. One man looked very like a policeman to me. Perhaps he had already heard about the little grave and had come to inspect it. They had nearly reached the juniper tree and I stumbled on behind but no one noticed me except the startled birds. They appeared to fly straight up from the ground, crying, "Chak-Chak-Chak," and there were three of them instead of two, and a great roaring came in my ears like a violent storm and the birds seemed to swoop towards me, and one had a great round stone in its fearful beak which it let fall and I knew I was to be entirely crushed by it as I saw it spinning down towards me.

30

ACTUALLY the policeman had not come about the little grave, but something quite different. There was a well-known goldsmith in Hill Rise who made beautiful and expensive jewellery from precious metals and valuable stones. That morning when he was sitting in his workshop making a heavy golden chain he saw through the skylight a large bird sitting on his roof singing what seemed to him a very beautiful song. He stood up and went towards the street; but as he crossed the threshold he lost one of his slippers. But he went right into the middle of the street with one shoe on and one off, and in his left hand he held the golden chain and in his right the pincers he had been working with, and the sun was shining brightly on the street. The bird had come to the edge of the roof and he called to it: "Bird, how beautifully you sing," and the bird sang something like, "Kywill, Kywitt, chak-chak-chak." This pleased the goldsmith so much that he hardly noticed when the bird swooped down, snatched the glittering chain from his hand, carried it to the roof, pecked at it for a few moments, and then flew away towards some gardens at the back.

Several people, some of them in cars, saw this happen, and they were astonished. Some said one thing and some another: "It's a thieving jackdaw"; "No, it's too large, a magpie most likely"; "Of course it's a magpie, all black and white with a long tail." Someone else said it was definitely a parrot and a crowd started to collect, and the jeweller, who was a shy man, scuttled into his shop and shut the door. It was only then that he noticed he'd lost a slipper. When he'd retrieved his slipper, he went into the small yard at the back; but no golden chain glittered there or in his neighbour's yard. He telephoned the police and they sent round a most helpful young constable who knew quite a lot about birds and their habits. After he had written a description of the missing gold chain, the young policeman suggested that they call on some of the nearby houses that had large gardens, The owners of the first two houses they visited said that, although magpies sometimes settled on the trees in their gardens, they hadn't seen any recently; but the next house holder they asked was an elderly woman who knew of the Forbeses' magpies and directed them there. "There is a little girl, a very dark little girl, who feeds them with her own lips, and they have built the strangest nest. The lady who died was very fond of them too and called them her *elsters*. I watch them from my bathroom window and there seem to be three birds now, but I haven't seen any gold chains. It's the large house with a carved bear outside. You can't miss it."

So they came to our house, the policeman and the jeweller, and Bernard took them to the thicket, followed by the indignant Marline. They found the birds pecking at the gold chain just under the juniper tree and the disturbed birds flew into the sky, then swooped down towards me—and that was when I fell to the ground, twitching and moaning, not crushed by a stone, but by my poor disordered mind.

31

FOR A TIME I was in a coma—for several days, they told me. Then came a terrifying time when I was crying out but couldn't speak proper words and didn't know where I was or who I was for that matter. Sometimes, when the drugs wore off, I thought I might be in purgatory. Quite often there were looming forms bending over me and at first their voices hurt my ears; it was as if they were shouting through a megaphone. Occasionally there were people I'd once known, but I couldn't remember who they were. Later, a nurse told me that the first time I spoke clearly was when Bernard stood by my bed and, although I didn't know him, something twisted in my heart and I said: "I'd rather be married to a fox than you." Nonsense, but it was a step forward.

The worst step forward was when my memory returned, all misty at first, then horribly clear. I called out and said I must talk to someone about Johnny; I was very worried about him. Then such a sympathetic woman came and sat beside me and let me talk as much as I wanted, making notes as she listened. It was some time before I realized she was a policewoman. She had a copy of the letter I'd written to Bernard and asked if it were true. She wanted to know why I was so afraid of him. I told her the letter was true, although my mind was very disturbed when I wrote it, and I'd buried poor little Johnny to hide his body from Bernard until I'd destroyed myself. I tried to explain how he was about the child, so obsessed with him as if he were his dead wife. In the state I was in I couldn't tell him his son was dead and he'd died because I left the lid of the chest open. But even if he had died in any other way, I still couldn't have told Bernard; I'd far rather be dead myself.

Later, a policeman came to see me too and asked the same questions over and over again, but they were kind, these police people. At least they didn't seem to think I'd murdered Johnny. It was unlawful burying they were going on about. I didn't have to appear at the inquest or in a police court because they said I was unfit to plead, but it was decided that I was to have treatment in a mental hospital. That was better than going to prison, and I really needed treatment. It wasn't only the depression and despair that came from time to time, but my mind felt so muddled and bruised that I couldn't concentrate. Someone had arranged for me to have *The Times* delivered every day; it was nice to see it, but I couldn't read it. There was talk about ECT, but my mother and Bernard were against it and when I found out what it was I was glad I'd escaped such an unpleasant experience.

Sometimes I had hallucinations, perhaps due to the drugs I was taking. I'd see Johnny swinging on his swing right into my room, backward and forward, and I'd call to him but he wouldn't stop and I could still see him if I shut my eyes. Then there was the mackintosh woman, who only appeared in the evenings. She was about three-and-a-half feet high and made of rolled up rubbery mackintoshes, and although she had no eyes, skilfully arranged buttons gave her a kind of face. She crawled from under my bed and scuttled about the room, appearing to be very busy sweeping in the corners of the room although she had no visible brush—or hands, for that matter. The slightest sound sent her scuttling under my bed again and I'd imagine I could smell a rubbery smell. For a time she appeared almost every night and I could see her even in the dark.

My mother was a frequent visitor. I didn't recognize her at first, but when I did we talked quite a lot although I didn't take in everything and sometimes dozed off while she was talking. Marline was staying with her and they were getting on "like a house on fire," she said. She was planning to sell her house and everything in it and live in something very different. "I don't know what, but it must be different. When you have recovered, perhaps you will help me. No antiques, though. I want everything modern and very simple—no clutter, if you know what I mean."

Mary came, bringing a suitcase filled with clothes suitable for being mad in. She had been to the house and collected them. She said she had had quite a long talk with Mrs. Hicks, who was rather miserable and shocked but managing to "look after the master" on her own. She had also had a talk with Peter, who had given evidence at the inquest: "Very nice evidence. We all said what a caring mother you were, even Bernard, and he admitted neglecting you. Oh dear, I shouldn't run on like this. They warned me not to."

Mopping my eyes, I said, "It doesn't matter. It's Bernard I'm sorry for. Having to go through an inquest on top of everything else. And the publicity too. He's such a proud man."

Mary shrugged. "He'll survive," she said rather unfeelingly, then asked if he visited me.

"Not since I've been more normal. I don't think he could bear it. But he has long talks with the psychiatrist, and mother has seen him once or twice. They discuss me, I believe. Mary, do you think I'll ever be a normal woman and be independent and able to take decisions again? My mother wants me to help her find another house. I'd like that."

When Mary had gone, I lay on my bed and pulled my dressing-gown round me and looked up at the high window. There was only the changing sky and a torn and faded flag fluttering from a pole, so worn and bleached it looked like elderly knickers. I think the window was barred.

The following day I was taken with my two suitcases of clothes to a psychiatric hospital on the outskirts of London. Only some of the wards had bars at the windows and most of the patients were free, at least the ones I met. I had a bit of a relapse soon after I arrived and had to be drugged again, but after a week or two I felt more normal and gradually left my private room, at first with a nurse in attendance, then whenever I felt like it. There were televisions in the large wards but I found them confusing after the first few minutes, partly because some of the patients made strange noises as they watched. I preferred the transistor my mother bought me and listened to it a lot, particularly to concerts and plays.

Mother was becoming the kindest of women and seemed to like me much more now I was rather insane; perhaps I had been too independent before. We got on so well we even made jokes. Living with Marline seemed to have melted her heart. She said she loved having her, it had given her a new interest in life. I missed the child so much it was quite painful, we'd always been so close. Mother did bring her occasionally for short visits, just for tea in my room; but I didn't really like her seeing me in such a place and mother said the patients were so starved for family life, they almost mobbed her.

Bernard had not been to see me in the psychiatric hospital. The doctors may have thought it might upset me to see him because one day my special doctor asked how I felt about seeing Bernard, did I feel up to it? I said I thought it was time we had a talk because I was beginning to imagine all kinds of horrors. Although I had had a few brief notes from him, they were extremely cold. So it was arranged that Bernard was to come.

One of the visiting hairdressers attended to my hair and the nurses manicured my hands, which had done no work for weeks—even Miss May would have approved of them. They went through my clothes and chose the ones they considered the most becoming, then opened my jewel case. They fell at once on the pink topaz ring with its sparkling diamonds, my engagement ring, but I said, "No, no, put it away," and they exchanged glances. Sadly they shut the suitcases and put them back in the cupboard and the little party was over.

In the early afternoon Bernard came, looking as proud and handsome as ever, but far from happy. He said, "Poor child, you've lost a lot of weight," and put his arm round me for a moment; but he didn't kiss me so I knew it was definitely the end, particularly when he asked if he could sit down and chose a chair far away from me. He asked me trite questions. Was I comfortable? How did I feel? Was I satisfied with my treatment? That kind of thing. Suddenly my eye fell on some vases containing water the nurse had left for the flowers my husband would bring. She knew I liked to arrange the flowers myself. I said rather spitefully, "Bernard, the nurse will be disappointed you didn't bring me any flowers. Look at the vases she left, three, all different sizes."

Bernard appeared stricken. "My God, I'm sorry. I forgot about flowers with so much on my mind. Bella, I'm so miserable with Gertrude and Johnny both gone. There is nothing to live for, nothing. Going back to that house of memories is hell. I've put it up for sale, you know."

I said I didn't know and he said there were a lot of things I didn't know and spoke of my "mental instability" and not wanting to shock me, though he'd spoken to my mother about his plans. "I think you misjudged that woman, Bella."

Then he told me that we could never live together again; now Johnny had gone there was no point in it. He added he was most likely leaving the country, going to Brussels and becoming more or less a sleeping partner in the London gallery. Of course I'd still have my income as a director and there would be money from the sale of the house so that I could buy a place of my own, "something better than that little shop you used to live in. By the way, I was surprised when I saw that magnificent room of yours in the basement. Extraordinary I knew nothing about it."

I said, "Would you have been interested? Peter helped me make it, did you know?"

"Yes, so he told me. I'd no idea you were such friends. When I move on to Brussels he's starting up on his own. He should be all right; he has plenty of connections and is very good at his work. I offered to set him up in Brussels, but he preferred to stay here."

He unfolded himself from the uncomfortable hospital chair and stood beside me for a moment with his hand on my shoulder. "Well, I'm sorry things have turned out as they have, my dear, but I'll keep in touch and let you or your mother know what's happening."

He turned towards the door but before he could open it I caught him by the hand and cried, "We were happy in Brussels, weren't we, Bernard, and in Madrid too?"

We were standing close together but he freed his hand and moved away and said, "If you say so, dear. Yes, of course we were happy," and he was gone.

I thought how strange the room looked, as if the air had been burnt away. My hand went up to my scar as it used to, but I forced it down and I thought, "If he can start again, so can I. And I'll chop up Bernard's chair!"

The nurse came in with six bunches of carnations and said, "They are from your husband." He'd already forgotten that I disliked carnations.

I asked the nurse to arrange them. They had no scent at all.

32

CHRISTMAS came and went. It wasn't too bad being in a psychiatric hospital because everyone tried to make the best of it, particularly the nurses. I was recovering all the time and now worked in the hospital library and had long talks with my fellow patients. Some of the women were very odd but most of the men I met in the library appeared normal, but sad. Then I started to go home for the weekends—well, not home, but to my mother's house. She hated the house as much as I did by now, so we drove about looking for houses for sale and eventually found one we liked in Chiswick. It stood in a tree-lined road not far from the river, a large Victorian house with four floors and quite a big garden with a magnolia tree just coming into bud. Mother was very taken with the attics. They had already been converted into a self-contained flat and Marline and I would live in the lower two floors and the semi-basement could be let. It was the magnolia tree that decided me to buy the house—I'd so missed the one I'd planted in the Twickenham garden—the tree and the large rooms, some of them with parquet flooring and french windows leading to the garden. Bernard had already put a large sum in my bank, part of the proceeds of selling the Richmond house and my mother gave me £20,000 so we were able to buy the house without taking out a mortgage.

Although Bernard's house was already sold, my furniture and personal belongings were still locked up in Bella's room. This worried me a lot. It was frustrating being imprisoned in the hospital when there was so much to do and only the odd weekend to sort things out. It preyed on my mind so much that the drugs I was taking had to be increased and I was lectured by the doctors. Then dear Peter came to the rescue. He moved all my things to the Chiswick house and decorated it just as I wanted it, casting all his own work aside at an important time for him, when he was starting up on his own.

Then my mother had the good idea that we should let the basement to Peter, whom we knew and trusted, rather than to some stranger. He had no permanent place of his own yet and was sharing flats with various friends and was working under difficult conditions, so it all fitted perfectly. Mother came to love and depend on Peter and, later on, so did I.

It was spring when I left the hospital finally. Peter and Mary came to fetch me. I was really sorry to say goodbye to some of the doctors and nurses. They had been so kind to me and built me up into a human being again—I hoped a stronger and better one than I'd been before.

Marline and my mother were waiting for me in our new home. It was completely finished now, even the kitchen was stocked with food and a celebration lunch was laid out in the dining-room and drinks in the drawing-room. It was the first time I'd had my own drawing-room and dining-room; the ones in the Forbeses' house had never seemed like mine. There were a few things from there scattered about, things Bernard or Miss Rose had thought I'd need like linen, china, and carpets, also some really beautiful oriental rugs and, oddly enough, the two beds with the elaborate headboards. Everything else had been sold except the paintings and books and the trunks containing Gertrude's things. Peter said he'd given Bernard's special chair to Mrs. Hicks to save me the bother of chopping it up. No one mentioned what had happened to the gruesome old chest.

It was like entering a different world when I was shown mother's attic flat with its built-in furniture, fitted carpets and, in the ultra-modern kitchen and bathroom, tiled floors. The sitting-room was a bit stark, but the black leather buttoned chairs were more comfortable than they looked and there was a view of the river, which pleased my mother very much. It was very different from her Kilburn home, but she said it was exactly what she wanted.

After I'd become used to the joy of living in my own home I grew a little restless. I felt I needed part-time work, so Mary suggested I became a buyer for her. This suited us both and left me plenty of time to look after Marline and do the cooking. A sturdy miner's daughter, the mother of five children came in to do the cleaning. I kept in touch with Miss Rose and sometimes worked in the gallery when they needed extra help, and I became quite friendly with Bernard's partner, a wise, elderly Jew. Miss Rose always warned me if Bernard was around but that wasn't often. I think he dreaded a meeting, but liked to write from time to time and even ask my advice. At first I was upset when I saw the Belgian stamp and his writing on an envelope; but later on they meant little to me. It was the same with Stephen's letters from America; I'd leave them on the mantelshelf for days before I opened them. Sometimes the letters of my husband and ex-lover lay there together. I used to answer them eventually and should have missed them if they didn't come.

Besides the semi-basement we let Peter use one of the upstairs bedrooms that had a good light to do his restoring work in. The strange thing was that we seldom met on the stairs and, except on Sundays when we all ate together as a family, we didn't see much of him, but if anything went wrong, my car not starting for instance, he was always there to help. Sometimes, when he wasn't too busy, we went to sale rooms together and he helped me buy things for Mary and sometimes myself. Occasionally we went to a film or play together. I knew he was fond of me, but sometimes wondered if he liked Mary better. He quite often went to her flat in the evenings and she'd cut his straight fair hair, she'd do it rather well, too, and she'd been known to iron his shirts, and they'd share a bottle of wine together as she ironed. We were never intimate like that although I had known him for over five years. He told me that he used to watch Gertrude and me in the garden together and I remembered how we had once seen his pale face looking down from his high window. We called him the prince in the tower, which suited him very well. Mother said, "I hope we aren't going to lose that nice young man to Mary. The house wouldn't be the same without him." And she was quite right, it wouldn't.

One morning, when I delivered some things to Mary's stall, she said casually, "I'm thinking of going to Spain with Peter—Barcelona, then perhaps Madrid. We could visit the flea market, the Rastro, that Bernard wouldn't allow you to go to."

I said, "Yes, I'm sure you will enjoy yourselves," and went home very thoughtfully.

As I entered the house, I could hear some Scarlatti drifting up the basement stairs, so knew that Peter was working down there. I slowly followed the music down the stairs and there was Peter, his tall body bent over a frame he was gilding with gold leaf, the gold still hanging, all shaggy. When it was finished he put it in the sunny area to dry and then turned and saw me standing there very still.

I said, "Peter, is it true that you are going to Spain with Mary?"

He looked surprised. "Did she say I was? If so, it's the first I have heard of it." Then he suddenly smiled. He didn't smile often but when he did, his face really lit up. He asked, "Would you mind if I did?"

I snapped, "Would I mind? Of course I would." And then, for the first time, I realized how much he meant to me and I could see by his face that he felt the same about me. Later he told me that he had loved me for years, ever since he first saw me at the Forbeses' house, but I was always so engrossed with them he knew he hadn't a chance, and then there was my travesty of a marriage which gave him the chance to help in small ways.

"Small ways?" I said. "Bella's room would have been nothing if it hadn't been for you. I'm afraid I rather took your help for granted. You spoke for me at the inquest, so Mary said. Do you call that a small thing?"

Actually Mary was planning to go to Madrid, but not with Peter, with a man she had been in love with for years. He was married to a paraplegic wife and all they had was an occasional holiday together. It was strange that I'd known her for a number of years but never knew she had a lover before.

We settled into the house in Chiswick very well, with mother in her uncluttered flat and the rest of us below, living the lives that suited us. Marline was happy at home, going to a school she liked and the proud owner of a dog, a Welsh sheepdog which she spent a considerable amount of time training, but all it did was round up other people's dogs. Peter had all the work he wanted and after the first year had to take on an assistant. I tried trimming his hair but wasn't very good at it—mistakes in cutting show up so on straight hair—but I allowed no one else to iron his shirts. When Bernard and I had been living apart for two years we obtained a divorce and Peter and I were able to marry, which was just as well, because I'd already started a baby. It was really lovely being pregnant with a kind husband to look after me.

One day when Mary and I were talking over cups of coffee in my kitchen she asked me to see the contents of a small house that was being sold, then immediately corrected herself. "Oh no, you won't want to go, it's in Richmond."

"Of course I don't mind going to Richmond," I said. "There hasn't been any need to go, that's all. Tell me about it."

She said the house, or rather cottage, was in a little backwater off George Street and had belonged to an elderly couple who had died. The son had told her there were a few antiques she might be interested in. He mentioned a small collection of glass paperweights, china 1920 pierrots, Rockingham poodles, ships and birds in glass cases. Not wildly interesting, but worth seeing.

My car was being serviced, so I made the journey by train. Everything looked the same: the depot of derelict buses on the right as the train drew in; the bookstall and flower shop on my left as I was leaving the station; the pet shop and the shop we used to call "the useful shop," with a wonderful display of brass handles, knockers and knobs of all kinds. I soon came to the cottage I was looking for, one of a row with tiny gardens in front, and the bereaved son waiting outside with the door open behind him. My business with him was soon settled. I bought everything he offered, including some theatre tinsels of Victorian actors in their original frames, which I knew Mary would be pleased with, and he agreed to deliver them to her flat that evening. The furniture was already sold to a house clearer. It was particularly ugly Edwardian and had an unpleasant smell.

When I left the cottage the spring sun was shining and instead of turning back to the station I made my way towards Richmond Hill, glancing every now and then in the windows of once-familiar shops. Dickens and Jones were already displaying summer dresses, but at that moment clothes did not interest me because I was six months pregnant and growing larger every day. I left George Street and found I was being drawn towards the quieter streets at the back and then up the hill towards the old Forbes house, the place where I had felt so much I'd almost been burnt away, the place that had made me and nearly ruined me. As I stood outside, I could almost feel Gertrude's presence and see her beautiful, brave figure bending over the flowers. The carved bear still guarded the house. It seemed as if he recognized me with his cold stone eyes.

I felt a strong compulsion to see the back of the house, the wild garden and the thicket. In spite of all it brought back to me I could not resist the desire to revisit the thicket where Gertrude and I used to sit, and look again at the tree where the magpies had built their nest and used to watch us from above as they chattered, and at the juniper tree whose fruit Gertrude used to eat with such abandon and, finally, at the place where those things I would like to forget occurred.

I slowly walked down a side road where there used to be an iron gate leading into the far end of the garden. The gate was still there, but when I looked in, that part of the garden had disappeared. In its place stood a tall block of flats built in Victoria plum-coloured bricks and with a horribly permanent look. The entire spinney had been built over and only the formal part of the garden remained, though it was not so badly overlooked as it might have been because the windows facing it were small ones, lavatory windows perhaps.

The new owners of the house must have sold over half of the ground it was standing on. I wondered what kind of people they were and returned to have one more look at the unchanged front of the house. As I stopped outside the wrought-iron gates, the front door opened and a plump dark woman came out, followed by two handsome little boys. They looked like Arabs to me and were excitedly talking in a foreign language. The mother did not speak at all but gracefully scattered small pieces of bread from a brass bowl for the chirping sparrows that immediately appeared. The boys ran to the old bear; the largest one rode on its back and the little one fed him with crumbs intended for the birds. I was glad to see children living in the house again.

OTHER NEW YORK REVIEW CLASSICS

For a complete list of titles, visit www.nyrb.com.

* *Also available as an electronic book.*